FANTAIL BOOKS

END GAME

Kate Daniel

END GAME

FANTAIL

FANTAIL BOOKS

Published by the Penguin Group
Penguin Books Ltd, 27 Wrights Lane, London W8 5TZ, England
Penguin Books USA Inc., 375 Hudson Street, New York, New York 10014, USA
Penguin Books Australia Ltd, Ringwood, Victoria, Australia
Penguin Books Canada Ltd, 10 Alcorn Avenue, Toronto, Ontario, Canada M4V 3B2
Penguin Books (NZ) Ltd, 182–190 Wairau Road, Auckland 10, New Zealand

Penguin Books Ltd, Registered Offices: Harmondsworth, Middlesex, England

First published in the United States of America by HarperCollins 1993
First published in Great Britain by Fantail 1993
10 9 8 7 6 5 4 3 2 1

Printed in England by Clays Ltd, St Ives plc

To Tom and Martha Jennings

For friendship and music and chicory coffee
over ten years

Several people helped in the writing of this book. My Good friend Kevin O'Donnell, Jr., writer and football fan, helped fill many gaps in my knowledge about sports. Tammy Groth, a photography major at the University of Arizona, and my friend Karen Pope of Vancouver, Canada, advised me on photographic matters.

And finally, my special thanks to Detective Karen Wright of the Tucson Police Department, for advice on police procedures.

SWEETHEART

The flashing blue and red lights were beautiful. Jessie McAllister tried not to think about what they meant as she focused her camera. The blue was the purest of ice-blues, the red a brilliant crimson. In the fading twilight, the blood on the pavement looked like a pool of oil, all color drained from it by the lights rotating on top of the squad car.

She snapped the shutter, then moved around the end of the car for a closer look. Jessie had been on her way home when she'd passed the scene of the accident. She'd reached for her camera out of instinct. Since she'd gotten her first Instamatic for her eighth birthday, she'd taken pictures of everything. The old Mamiya she carried now had been given to her for Christmas her junior year of high school, and she always carried it. But she'd never taken pictures of a

1

fatal accident before. She didn't know what had happened; there were no wrecked cars nearby, but a still form lay in the gutter, with books spilling from a backpack on the ground. Jessie took a picture of the bag, wondering if the victim had also been a student at the university.

Jessie took another shot, multiple shadows caused by all the different lights. As a photography major at the University of Arizona, she knew that good pictures could turn up anyplace, and some of them would be ugly. Jessie noticed she wasn't the only one there with a camera. A police photographer was moving around, getting shots of the scene from several angles. His flash unit lit up the body of the young woman briefly, and Jessie looked away. She couldn't bring herself to take pictures of something that gruesome.

The normally busy street was blocked off and people swarmed around the victim, busy with the aftermath of tragedy. Several police squad cars lined the road, all with flashers going, along with a van marked "Tucson Police Department." An ambulance stood nearby, but the three paramedics beside it weren't doing anything; it was too late for this victim. A yellow plastic tape had been strung around a section of the street, with the words "Police/Fire Line—Do Not Cross" stamped in black letters along the length of it. Inside the perimeter of the tape a tired-looking man in a gray suit looked down at the body, while another paramedic knelt beside it. Behind the man in the suit a uniformed officer laughed at something someone had said. Jessie focused on the contrasting expressions and clicked the shutter again. The tired man looked up at the flash, and his eyes met Jessie's briefly, then he bent over to speak with the paramedic. Tire marks—streaks of burnt rubber—led away from the body, swerving from the curb, then continuing for a few feet. The police tape paralleled them. Jessie got a shot of the black lines and curb framed by the tape. As she did, the police photographer knelt down beside her and took a picture of the marks as well.

Behind her she could hear a distraught woman's voice. ". . . just came right *at* her!" The voice dissolved into sobs. Jessie turned. A couple dressed in jogging suits stood just outside the taped area, speaking to a woman dressed in slacks and a warm-looking windbreaker. The jogger was crying, her partner's arm around her. As they spoke, the other woman made notes. The trio didn't look around when Jessie's flash went off. Twilight had faded from the sky, and she shivered, realizing how cold it had become. Even in Arizona, January nights are cold, and the sharp wind was cutting through Jessie's University of Arizona sweatshirt.

Jessie turned away from the joggers to retrieve her bike, which she'd parked by a tree, then stopped again. Paramedics were wheeling a stretcher toward the body. She raised her camera to take one final picture of the end of the drama—the paramedics at work—when she froze. Through her telephoto lens, she could see the face of the victim. And it looked familiar.

Jessie stared. With fumbling hands she automatically snapped the lens cap back onto her camera and zipped it into its case. Jessie moved along the tape until she was directly opposite the body and, for the first time, looked at the sightless eyes. Her throat suddenly dry, Jessie ducked under the tape. It was Laurie.

Before she could get any closer, a hand grasped her upper arm. "Back behind the tape, miss," said a firm voice. The woman who'd been questioning the witnesses stepped in front of her and continued, "It's there for a reason. Now if you'll just move back . . ." The woman broke off as Jessie continued to stare at Laurie. The crew from the ambulance spread a blanket over the body, cutting off the nightmarish sight of that dead gaze. Jessie shuddered.

The woman's official tone of voice shifted slightly. "Do you recognize her?" At Jessie's faint nod, she said, "I think we'd better ask you some questions." She raised her voice slightly. "Ramon?"

The man in the gray suit broke away from the group around the corpse and joined them. "What you got, Mary?" There was a flash of recognition in his face as he frowned at Jessie's camera case. "Newspaper?"

"No." Jessie swallowed hard. "Is that—I think that's Laurie Birkson. Is it?"

"That's what the ID says," he said. "Did you know her?" He motioned to one of the uniformed police offi-

4

cers standing nearby and spoke with him in a low voice. Jessie couldn't keep her eyes off the small group around the body. Around *Laurie*. The body, now wrapped in a blanket, was being carefully slipped into a large bag. *Body bag*, she thought. *That's what they call those things. Laurie is in a body bag.*

"You all right, miss?" The officer's hand was under her elbow as Jessie turned away from the grim scene. Jessie realized she was dizzy. She nodded—a tiny gesture that moved her head less than an inch—and found her voice again.

"I'm fine." Her voice shook as she spoke.

"I'm Detective Gutierrez," the man in the gray suit said, "and this is Detective Peters. Would you take a look at this, please?" He held out an open wallet, and Jessie glanced down at it. An Arizona driver's license was in the plastic holder.

"Yes, that's her." This time her voice almost sounded normal. "Laurie Birkson. She's in my English class."

"You a student? Your name, please?" the detective asked.

Jessie noticed that he was jotting her answers down in a small notebook. She gave her name and address, and added, "We're both freshmen. I think Laurie's from Yuma; I don't know her that well. She works at the library." The words rang in her ears as Jessie realized they were wrong. Laurie *had* worked at the library. She wouldn't any longer. And now Jessie would never get to know her.

5

He grunted, a noncommittal sound. "That matches the license. Did you see it happen?"

Jessie shook her head. "I'm not even sure what happened. Hit-and-run?" He grunted again, and she went on. "I was riding home—I work at Sweeny's."

"Riding?" She pointed at her bike on the sidewalk. It had fallen on its side.

"When did you recognize her?" The question was abrupt, and Jessie realized the police must have been here for some time, asking questions of everyone who'd witnessed the hit-and-run. He probably wondered why she hadn't said anything sooner. She explained, emphasizing that she hadn't been focusing on the body in her pictures. It was only when she had gotten a clear enough look at the face that she'd realized who it was. Jessie swallowed hard. She didn't like to remember that terror-filled face, or those vacant eyes.

He seemed to accept her explanation. Glancing at her camera again, he changed the subject. "What were you taking all the pictures for?"

"I'm majoring in photography," she answered. "And Mr. Sweeny—I told you I work at Sweeny's Studio—Mr. Sweeny keeps telling me I should always have my camera ready." She broke off. "I wasn't taking pictures of—of Laurie, I told you that. Just the people, and the lights, and the ambulance, and everything." She waved her hand, indicating all the activity around them.

"Yeah." Detective Gutierrez nodded and shut the notebook. Behind him, the stretcher with the bag containing Laurie was being wheeled into an unmarked minibus. Ambulances were for the living. "All right. Thanks for your cooperation, but next time you see a police tape, stay behind it. See Miss McAllister back to her bicycle, Mary." He smiled slightly. "Ride carefully, miss." The smile faded as he turned away. Detective Peters nodded and led Jessie back to the edge of the taped-off area.

Jessie felt sick. She'd seen dead animals alongside the road, and once she'd seen a car hit a dog. She'd been to a few funerals, where the dead people were made up to look as if they were asleep. But she'd never seen anything like this. Laurie's face had been untouched, but the rest of her—death had left Laurie crumpled and bloody. This wasn't like a funeral, where the body looked as artificial as a store mannequin. It was real.

By the time she reached the apartment building five blocks away, Jessie was shaking all over. She managed to fasten the chain lock on her bike. Then she headed for the apartment. Before she reached the door, it was pulled open from inside by her roommate, Valerie King.

"Jessie, where've you been?" her roommate asked. "The show starts in forty-five minutes!" Light spilled out of the apartment around Val, making a halo of her short blond hair. She was already dressed, Jessie noted

7

with a pang, wearing the lapis-blue sweater she'd bought the week before and her matching blue dangle earrings. Val looked great, and she knew it. Jessie had forgotten all about the double date they had planned for the evening. She felt grubby, and she wanted to take a shower. There wasn't any blood on her, but she felt as though she were covered in it.

The guys were already there. The apartment always seemed smaller with two huge football players in it. Val's date, Art Ducas, straddled a kitchen chair backward. Randy Beckman, Jessie's boyfriend, came and greeted her with a hug. As they walked into the living room, he put his arm around her waist.

"Something's the matter," Randy stated. "What happened?" He sank onto the couch, pulling her with him, his arm tightening around her slightly.

"I'm late," Jessie said.

Art crossed his arms on the back of the chair and looked at her. Val's boyfriend was so big, the ordinary kitchen chair looked as if it had come from a dollhouse. "No joke. What kept you?"

Jessie could still see the expression on Laurie's face as she said, "There was an accident over on Fourth Avenue, just down from the studio. Hit-and-run. I didn't see it happen, but I got there while the cops were asking people questions, and I—I recognized who it was. It was Laurie Birkson. She's dead."

"Dead!" The exclamation burst from Val.

"I told them I knew her, and they asked me about a

8

million questions." Jessie stopped as she gave way to the shakes once more.

"Easy," Randy said. His large hands moved with surprising delicacy as he stroked Jessie's dark hair. "Anybody'd be shook up, seeing someone they know like that. Do the cops have any idea who did it?"

Jessie shook her head, not trying to speak.

"I know her—*knew* her—enough to say hi, but that's about all," Val said. "Mostly from the library. Didn't you say she was in your English class, Jessie?"

"She *was* in my English class," Jessie said, "but she was a photography major, too. She was in my art survey course last semester, and I've seen her around the center."

"You want to just forget about going out tonight?" Randy asked, still stroking her hair.

"I don't even want to move off this couch," Jessie said.

"I don't blame you," Val said. "We can see the movie some other time."

"I didn't know her," Art remarked. "But if you don't want to go out, that's cool."

Val turned to him. "You must have known her, Art. The redhead who worked on the main desk at the library? Brenda's friend?"

He shook his head. "She may have known your ex-roommate, but that doesn't mean I knew her," he said. "There're a lot of people working at the library. Who knows who they are?"

The University of Arizona was a big school, with a total enrollment larger than the population of Jessie's hometown, Bisbee. Laurie had been majoring in the same subject as Jessie, yet they'd shared only a couple of classes and had hardly known each other. They liked some of the same photographers and had shared English assignments. That was about it. Art was right; there were way too many people on campus to know them all.

"All right, so you don't want to go out," Art said. "But let's do something, not just talk about her."

Val made popcorn, and they put a video on, but Jessie couldn't shake the memory. The guys left early, and she went to bed. With luck, she wouldn't have nightmares about Laurie.

Jessie went directly to Sweeny's Studio next morning. She had only two classes on Fridays, but she was cutting to go with her boss on a shoot. Jack Sweeny had been hired to take pictures at the Desert Museum for a new fund-raising campaign, and he was taking Jessie along as his assistant. He was an old friend of her father's, which was how she'd gotten the job at the studio. Jobs at a good studio like Sweeny's were always at a premium, and freshmen didn't normally get a chance at them.

Jessie arrived at Sweeny's an hour early, since she wanted to develop the pictures she'd taken the night before. Like many studios, Sweeny's sent color film out to be developed, but had a darkroom for processing black-and-white work. By the time Jack was ready to leave for the museum, the pictures were finished. Jessie took the prints along, intending to show them to Jack later.

Jack flipped on the radio as soon as they got into the Jeep. Jessie hated the station, one that played light rock, but it was Jack's Jeep and he was the boss. As they headed west, Jack began telling her what they'd be doing and why jobs such as this were worth more than the amount they paid. He was fond of lecturing, and Jessie usually enjoyed it. But right now her mind was on the photos of Laurie, and she wasn't listening. As they passed the interstate, the music stopped and was followed by a newscast. Jessie leaned forward, listening closely to the report. After a few minutes there was a story about the hit-and-run. The police hadn't found the driver of the murder vehicle.

Murder? The newscast continued, saying witnesses—Jessie thought of the joggers—had told police the car had deliberately headed for the victim. The car, which had been reported stolen, had been found a half mile away, the keys still in the ignition.

Jessie stared ahead, seeing nothing of the mountains in front of her. "Murder" was a word on the news or TV cop shows. It wasn't a word to use about people, real people, people she knew. The joggers must have been mistaken. The sudden silence as the radio was turned off broke Jessie's daze, and she realized Jack had

11

spoken to her a couple of times.

"Sorry, Mr. Sweeny." She looked over at him. "What'd you say?"

"What I was saying before can wait," he said. "That story hit you pretty hard. Someone you knew?"

Jessie nodded. "Yeah, but that's not all. I *saw* it." As they started the steep climb up to Gates Pass, she told him about the shock of seeing a dead body, the double shock of realizing she knew the person, and taking pictures of the whole thing.

"And that was why you were in early, huh?" He slowed for the first of the sharp bends as the road twisted up the canyon. "Get any good shots?"

Jessie's hand groped automatically for the handle on the dash as she leaned against the curve. "I think so. I've got them with me. I was planning to ask you to look at them later."

"I don't want to right now, that's for sure." He downshifted as they climbed again, stuck behind a tourist in a motor home with out-of-state plates.

"Snowbirds," Jack muttered, referring to the tourists. Such vehicles had no business on this road; it was too narrow and dangerous, but some people always tried it. They reached a short, straight stretch, and with a sigh of relief Jack managed to pass the motor home. "Remind me to take a look at your pictures when we get done at the museum. Any shots of your friend, what was her name—Laura?" They slowed for the sharp bend that marked the top of the pass. It was a tight squeeze, with steep cliffs falling away on the other side.

"Laurie," Jessie corrected him. "No, I didn't recognize her at first, but I didn't want to take pictures of a corpse."

"Take the pictures. Always take the pictures. If you decide later you don't want them, fine, you can throw them out, but if you don't take them and then decide you want them, you're out of luck. That's one of the most important things you have to learn, Jessie." She had triggered one of his favorite lectures. She'd heard it a hundred times since she'd started work at the studio last fall. It was good advice, too, but this time Jessie didn't concentrate. Instead, as he spoke, she pulled out the pictures and looked at them once more. Here were the tire marks, the stark shadows cast by the bright lights, the joggers arm in arm as the woman wept and Detective Peters quietly took notes.

A detail in one picture—the backpack spilled into the gutter—caught her eye, and she looked at it more closely. A small stuffed animal any student at the university would recognize was halfway out of the bag. It was the Wildcat, the mascot of the University of Arizona. But this one had on a miniature football jersey with the number 27 on it. Jessie had a similar one in her room, number 63. It was Randy's; the Wildcats team had been presented with these special Wildcats earlier in the month, at the end of a successful season. The Alumni Association had had them specially

13

made. Each one had one player's number on it, and they'd made a big deal of presenting them at the banquet. They were supposed to be unique.

Jessie stared at the picture, puzzled. The night before, Art had said he didn't know Laurie. But 27 was Art's number.

For the rest of the day, the question nagged at Jessie. Art had been so definite when he said he didn't know Laurie. But the Alumni Association had made such a big deal about the Wildcat dolls being one of a kind. Although Randy had given his to Jessie, Art had told Val he was keeping his as a good-luck charm for when he hit the pros. Why had Laurie had it?

Jessie thought that if someone had started to make copies, Art's number would surely be used. He was an all-American in both his sophomore and this year. From what Val said, there was a chance he wouldn't graduate next spring. Professional teams were already interested in him, and he might get a contract before he finished his senior year next fall. Art was smart, but he didn't bother much about classes. Not like Randy. Randy had a football scholarship, but he wasn't a first-string player, and his number would never show up on mass-produced souvenirs. His real love was botany, his major, and he planned to go on to graduate school. His grades were so high that he probably could have gotten a scholarship without football.

The Arizona-Sonora Desert Museum was one of Jessie's favorite places. Despite the name, it was a zoo and an arboretum combined; the exhibits were living plants and animals and birds. She had her camera with her, but she wouldn't be using it much on this trip. She was here to help Jack. The ads for the new campaign focused on the desert cats, and they spent most of the day trying to get one jaguar to cooperate. He ignored them as they took shot after shot, lowering his head to lick his hindquarters or stopping to scratch a flea each time they thought they had a perfect picture.

"I've got some great pictures here, but I doubt if they're what the committee wants for the brochures," Jack said with a grin at one point. "I don't think he wants his picture taken."

Jessie laughed. "Maybe he's like my nephew," she said. "I had to take pictures of his Cub Scout troop once. They loved it. That was the problem, they didn't want to settle down. Inanimate objects are a lot easier to photograph," Jessie said lightly. Then she sobered as she thought of the pictures she'd taken the night before. *Some* inanimate objects were easier.

By the time they finished shooting the jaguar, Jessie had shaken off the images that lingered in her mind. The drive back to the studio seemed much shorter than the one that morning. They discussed the animals, the light, the composition of the shots, and Mr. Sweeny got in another of his standard lectures, this one on the combination of art and business. Just because she would spend most of her professional life doing commercial photography didn't mean Jessie wouldn't need to strive for high standards.

When they got to the studio, he promptly used her own photos as examples. Sorting through her shots from the night before, he ignored Jessie's discomfort and critiqued each photograph. For example, he told her, the tire tracks were an interesting composition, but nothing unusual as a single shot and not worth trying to sell. When Jessie said she hadn't thought about selling any of them, he shook his head.

"Jessie, you didn't take them for the market, but that doesn't mean you can't sell them. Always, if there's a market for your work, go ahead and sell it. You can't afford to turn up your nose at getting paid. No photographer can." He held up the shot of the joggers talking to Detective Peters. "Now, take this one. It's a good composition, but it's nothing unique. It's a typical crying-witnesses photo.

"Now this one is the best shot—" He held up a dramatic shot of the pool of blood, crisscrossed by shadows from the squad car's flashers. Jessie winced. "All right, it makes you uncomfortable. But look at it." She did, and she had to admit he was right. It was a good photograph. Somehow that made it worse. "Put this one in your portfolio, but no newspaper will buy it. Too 'arty,' and there's no obvious subject."

Despite herself, Jessie was looking at the photos with a fresh eye now, analyzing them professionally. She paused at the one of the backpack. "How about this one?" she asked. She didn't tell Mr. Sweeny why she found it interesting. "Hmmm." He took it from her and studied it. "Nope, I doubt if they'd want it. It's a good personal look at the victim, but it might be *too* personal."

By the time they finished sorting through the photos, he had discarded most of them. Out of the entire stack there were only half a dozen he thought might be salable. They all showed people working around the body.

"It's not too late," he said, glancing up at the clock. "Come on, I'll take you."

"Take me where?" Jessie asked, startled.

"What have we been talking about?" Mr. Sweeny sounded irritated. "The newspaper, of course. You can't expect them to come here to buy your photos. Come on."

"But . . ." Jessie thought the lecture had been theoretical, but a few minutes later they were heading south to the main offices of one of Tucson's newspapers. It was the first time she'd tried to sell any of her work.

And they bought one of the photos.

* * *

The next morning Jessie spent a long time looking at the *Arizona Daily Star*. They had a big follow-up article about Laurie's death on the front page of the second section, and they had used Jessie's photo. It showed Detective Gutierrez staring at Laurie's body, while a uniformed policeman laughed. All that was visible of the body was one arm.

"The cops probably won't like this one very much," the editor who had purchased the photo had said with a grin. "Makes for a nice, lively paper, though." It was a good photo, and it drew attention to the article.

Monday was Jessie's heaviest class day, and she had extra assignments in math and English. Her math instructor didn't care about cuts if she could do the work, but she had to make up everything she'd missed on Friday. After her final class, she headed for the library. She had research to do for her art survey class, and it was a better place to study than the apartment. The guys in the next unit usually had their stereo blasting all day.

She chose a quiet nook on the third floor, dumped her books on the low table, and curled up in a comfortable chair. There were more conventional tables and chairs nearby, but the shabby old armchairs, like the ones in the family room at home in Bisbee, always made her feel relaxed. It had been a rough day.

Jessie had immediately felt the impact of the empty seat near her in freshman comp. It wasn't as though Jessie had been very good friends with Laurie, but she'd seen Laurie's body. It made Jessie feel closer to her than she had while Laurie had been alive. *Murder.* It didn't feel real. But she was here to study, not to brood. She reached for her art survey book.

She was deep in a section on the paintings of Tintoretto when she heard her name. "Hi, Jessie. Got a minute?"

She looked up. It was Brenda Wolinsky. Jessie regarded her warily but said, "Sure." She pushed the books on the table to one side with her foot, making room for Brenda's armful.

Brenda had roomed with Val the year before. They were both sophomores. The two had gotten along all right during their freshman year, but they'd spent most of the first semester this year fighting, and shortly before Thanksgiving break, Brenda had moved out. Jessie had been renting an apartment by herself, but it was more than she could afford. When Val asked her to move in after Brenda left, Jessie had promptly said yes. Even with her job at Sweeny's, living alone off campus was just too expensive.

Jessie didn't know what had caused the fights, but she could guess. Conversation with Brenda was like a debate even when she agreed with you, and when she disagreed, it was like a war. Arguing was her hobby. That and gossip.

"You heard about Laurie Birkson, didn't you?" Brenda asked.

"Yeah." Jessie didn't intend to tell Brenda about actually having been at the scene of the crime.

"I'm pretty upset about it," Brenda confided. "I liked Laurie."

"I didn't know you knew her."

"Yeah, I did," Brenda said. She dropped into the chair beside Jessie's. "It's funny—this is such a big school, you never think about knowing anyone unless you have classes with them. It's surprising who knows each other sometimes."

"I never thought much about it," Jessie said. Brenda gave her a crooked little smile. "Anyway, I hope the cops find out who did it."

"That was what I wanted to ask you about. Have they questioned Art yet?"

"Art?" Jessie was surprised. "I don't know, but why would they want to?"

"Well, he was dating her," Brenda said. She pushed a short strand of limp blond hair behind her ear and looked at Jessie, her face filled with malicious delight. "Didn't you know? I'm pretty sure Val doesn't. I haven't heard an explosion. But I'm surprised Randy didn't tell you."

Jessie sat up straight in the chair. "What do you mean? Art's been dating Val since last year."

"Sure, but you know what jocks are like. He's not as committed as Val likes to believe." Brenda shrugged. "Val's going to have to wake up one of these days. But I wish Laurie had steered clear of him. I figured she'd get hurt."

21

She wasn't hurt, she was killed, Jessie thought numbly. But that couldn't be what Brenda meant. "Art said he didn't know her."

"Yeah, right." Brenda snorted. "Like he's really going to admit he had anything to do with a murder victim. Laurie'd found out some stuff about Mr. Hotstuff Jock, and she could have gotten him thrown off the team if she hadn't been crazy about him. You think he's going to want to talk about that?"

"What sort of stuff?" Jessie asked, curiosity getting the better of her.

"Steroids." Brenda made the word ominous, but Jessie shook her head. Jessie had read that the drugs sometimes added muscle at the expense of mental and physical health. Everyone always accused football players of using steroids illegally, but Jessie didn't believe Art was using them.

"Give me a break," Jessie said. "Those things can be too dangerous. Art knows better than that."

"Look at his size—" Brenda began.

"He's a football player," Jessie interrupted her. "And I've seen him eat." She grinned. "Randy, too, for that matter. Between them, those two eat enough in a day to feed a family for a week."

"It's more than just food," Brenda said. "Besides, he's got a mean temper."

Jessie didn't bother to answer that time. If a bad temper was proof of steroids, an awful lot of people were using them.

"Anyway, I figure it's not going to take long for the cops to find out about his dating Laurie," Brenda went on, returning to the original subject. "Val'll go ballistic when she hears about it. It should be entertaining."

Jessie looked at her watch and jumped up. "Hey, I'm going to be late for class," she exclaimed as she hurriedly gathered her books off the table. "Catch you later." She didn't have a class, but she'd had enough of Brenda. No wonder Val hadn't been able to stand living with her. Val might not be a perfect roommate, but at least she didn't gossip. Jessie ran down the stairs and out of the library.

She unlocked her bike from the rack and began pedaling away. Brenda made everything sound so nasty. Even if Art *had* been dating Laurie—

A horn honked, and Jessie skidded sideways as she braked. "Hey, watch where you're going!" a voice snarled. She got the bike under control and looked around. It was Art; she'd nearly ridden right in front of him.

He pulled his red convertible over and stopped in a No Parking zone. He had lost the snarl when he saw Jessie. Now he grinned at her mockingly from the car. "I don't want to run over you, Jessie, you might scratch the paint." The restored '68 Mustang was his pride and joy. "You must have been thinking about Randy."

"Just about classes," she said quickly.

"Classes? Why're you wasting time thinking about *that*?" He grinned again and suggested some better

23

things to think about that left Jessie hot with embarrassment. He seemed to find her reaction funny.

"Yeah, well, some of us *have* to worry about classes. But there was something else as well." Jessie hesitated, then unslung her backpack and balanced it on the handlebars of her bike. The conversation with Brenda had her curiosity at fever pitch. She dug in the side pocket of her backpack and took out the photo. "Do you remember my telling you about the pictures I took the other night? This was one of them." She handed Art the picture.

He glanced at it, then handed it back. "So it's a backpack full of books. Isn't that sort of morbid, carrying around pictures of dead people's things?"

Jessie ignored his comment. She pointed to the figure of the mascot, half-concealed by the edge of the bag but with the number clearly visible. "Isn't that your Wildcat, Art? I thought you said you didn't know Laurie."

"I didn't, dammit." He scowled and reached for the photo as Jessie started to put it away. "Give me that thing!" He caught hold of one edge, and the picture ripped in half.

She yelped, and he pulled his hand back sharply. Then he handed her the half picture with a laugh. "That takes care of that. Look, I said I didn't know her. Maybe I saw her at the library, how the hell should I know? What difference does it make, anyway?"

Jessie smoothed the halves of the torn photograph

together with her fingertips, then slipped them between the pages of a book in her backpack. It didn't really matter; she could make another print from the negative. "I was just curious," she said. "It's your number, after all, and it sure looks like one of the ones they gave you guys at the banquet."

He scowled. "Well, it isn't. I kept mine. Look, get off my case, will you?" He peeled away from the curb without another word, cutting abruptly across the street to the parking garage. There was a squeal of brakes as he cut off another car, but he didn't even glance toward it, ignoring the driver's shouts.

She shrugged the pack back on. Halfway to the corner, she looked back and stopped again. He had come out of the garage and was crossing the street. Brenda had come out of the library and was on an intersecting path with Art. Fascinated, Jessie watched to see what would happen. Considering the way the girl had been talking about Art earlier, Jessie couldn't imagine why she wanted to talk to him, but she had stopped him. Even though Art was at least a foot taller, Brenda seemed to dominate the conversation. His handsome face twisted into a scowl, and he shook his head at whatever she'd said. He started walking toward the library again, with Brenda following, still talking. They vanished around a corner. Slowly Jessie rode on, wondering what Brenda had been saying to Art. It couldn't be what she'd said in the library, surely.

The apartment was almost two miles from the library, on the other side of campus. The late-January sky was a clear chilly blue, and the air held just enough nip to make riding a bike enjoyable exercise. Jessie took her time getting home, thinking about Brenda. The girl seemed so determined to stir up trouble for Art. Or was she just still mad at her ex-roommate, Valerie?

When Jessie got back to the apartment, Val was doing her nails. "Randy called," she said, waving her right hand in the air to dry the polish. "He said he'll pick you up at seven. Were you going to borrow my sweater?"

Jessie glanced at the clock. It wasn't even five yet. She had plenty of time. "I don't think so, thanks. You going out?"

"I'm not sure," Val said as she started doing the nails on her left hand. "Art's coming over." She smiled up at Jessie briefly. "If you're going out with Randy, maybe Art and I will just stay here."

"I saw Brenda at the library," Jessie said, changing the subject to the one she'd been thinking about the entire way home. "She was upset about Laurie."

"A lot of people are, but I doubt if Brenda's one of them," Val said. "Not unless Laurie was a busybody like Brenda is. If Laurie helped her spread rumors, Brenda *might* be upset about it. She wouldn't care otherwise."

Brenda and Val had parted on such bad terms,

there was no use talking to either of them about the other. Jessie hadn't really known Val then; they'd met through the guys. After she'd started dating Randy, she had slowly gotten to know a number of the other football players and their girlfriends.

Jessie did venture one more comment about Brenda. "She was saying something about Art—"

"I'll bet she was!" Val's temper flared. "She was always saying something about him, or to him, trying to start fights for us. Art's *my* boyfriend! Not just a boyfriend." Val took a deep breath and calmed down, though her eyes still reflected her anger. "Look, Jessie, anything that little witch says about me or Art you can just ignore. She was jealous from the first time Art took me out."

Jessie got ready for her date. She put on a bright yellow sweater of her own, rather than the new blue one Val had offered to lend her. The blue was pretty, but it didn't match her dark coloring as well as the vivid yellow. By the time Jessie finished her makeup, Val's temper had evaporated, and she had also finished getting dressed, in a simple shirt and jeans and a ton of jewelry.

To Jessie's relief, Randy got there before Art. After the ugly little scene over the photograph, she didn't want to run into him again for a while. They drove over to their favorite pizza place, and by the time the food arrived, Jessie had forgotten about the encounter. After the pizza, they went to a movie. It was almost midnight by the time the show let out. They walked back to the car, arms around each other. The clear day had turned into a frosty night. Jessie was glad when they reached the car and Randy got the heater going. For a while they drove around talking.

"Randy, do you know if Art knew Laurie?" Jessie asked, when the conversation turned again to the accident.

"He said he didn't, that night when you—when it happened," Randy said. Jessie noticed he hadn't given her a direct answer. "Why? I mean, how come you're asking?"

"Something Brenda said this afternoon." Briefly Jessie repeated Brenda's accusations about Art cheating on Val and described her own run-in with Art later. She finished, "All right, maybe Val's right and Brenda's just jealous or something, but he sure acted funny when I asked him. And there's the picture. That little stuffed Wildcat looked just like the ones they gave you guys on the team, and I know Art didn't give his to Val. So I wondered."

"Did you ask Val?"

"Not really. I told her Brenda had been gossiping about Art, but she acted like that was normal."

"That's no joke," Randy muttered. There was silence in the car for a few minutes except for the tape player; then he sighed. "Look, I didn't like it, but I figured it wasn't any of my business when Art said he didn't know Laurie. I wasn't going to call him a liar in front of Val. But he shouldn't have dragged me into his lies, especially if he's lying to you. He may operate that way, but I don't intend to." Randy parked the car in front of the apartment and turned to Jessie. "You can decide on your own whether or not to tell Val. You know her better than I do; it's your call."

"Tell her what?" Jessie asked. She was sure by now that she knew, but she wanted to clear away all the hints and lies.

"For once, Brenda's right. Art didn't just know Laurie, he'd been dating her on the sly. He hadn't told Val yet, but I think he was ready to dump her for Laurie."

"Then why . . ." Jessie started.

"Why didn't he say anything?" Randy shrugged. "Maybe he didn't want to upset Val. He likes her, he just doesn't want to be tied down yet, and she does."

"He didn't have to lie."

"I guess he thought he did," Randy said uncomfortably. "I can't tell him what to do. Question is, what are you going to do now? You going to tell Val?"

Jessie frowned slightly as she considered this. It was true: Val would be hurt and angry. Maybe there was no point, now that Laurie was dead. It might be cold-blooded to look at it that way, but would it do Laurie any good if Val and Art broke up now? Maybe she should just let Art make the next move. He was still inside the apartment with Val; his car was parked in front of the building.

"I guess not," she said slowly. "Like you said, it'd upset Val. But I don't want him lying to me anymore about it, either."

"He won't," Randy promised. "I'll tell him you know. I think he's asking for trouble, myself, but like I said, I can't run his love life for him." He smiled at Jessie. "I'm more interested in my own, anyway." He pulled her closer to demonstrate his interest. After a while Jessie heard the roar of the Mustang's engine behind her as Art left.

The Tucson police were housed in a building a few blocks away from the rest of the city buildings. Jessie hesitated outside, wondering how she would find Detective Gutierrez.

The paper that morning hadn't had anything new about Laurie. Reading through the brief article, Jessie had recalled her conversation with Brenda. Gossip or not, Brenda had been right about one thing. If the police were checking up on what Laurie had been doing before she died, they should know about Art. But he had lied to Val, and he might have lied to the police as well. And they might not have realized what the Wildcat meant. Jessie already believed that she was inextricably involved in this murder case, and she wanted to know what the police were doing.

A policewoman in uniform was behind a window like a bank teller's near the door, and Jessie stepped over to her.

"Can I see Detective Gutierrez?" she asked.

"Is he expecting you?" The woman asked a series of swift questions, determining what Jessie's business was, then made a phone call. After exchanging a few sentences with someone, the policewoman said, "He'll be down in a few minutes. You can come in." The policewoman pressed a button unlocking the door.

There was a large lobby, with chairs and couches, and relics of Tucson's police history in cases along the walls. In a few minutes the elevator opened and Detective Gutierrez stepped out. He still looked tired, Jessie thought. Maybe he always did.

"Miss McAllister? You have some new information?" He gave her an assessing look. It wasn't hostile, but Jessie wondered why he seemed so wary. "Why don't we go up to an interview room and talk?" He led the way back to the elevator, and she followed, feeling slightly intimidated.

They entered a small room, with a table and plastic chairs that could have come from any school cafeteria. "Have a seat. Coffee?" If the routine was designed to put her at ease, it didn't work completely, but she felt a little less tense as she sipped at the scalding coffee. The coffee was horrible, but at least it was hot. She'd had a long ride, and the weather was chilly. She took another swallow, almost burning her tongue.

"I took some pictures the night Laurie died," she said, getting the print out of her purse, "and I wondered if you'd noticed this." She laid the photo on the table

33

in front of the detective, but he didn't even glance at it.

"I remember the pictures," he said. "You claimed you were just taking them for practice or something. Then—look what shows up in the paper yesterday." He opened a folder lying on the table and pulled out a clipping from the *Arizona Daily Star*. His finger poked at the photo she'd sold to the paper, and he added, "You also said you weren't with the newspaper, and the paper doesn't usually buy outside photos. Care to explain?"

"Explain what?" Jessie was bewildered. It was a good photo. She couldn't see why it had Gutierrez upset. "I didn't plan on selling any pictures, but my boss thought I should try, and the paper liked this one. What's wrong with it?"

"Your boss? Yeah, that's right, you said you worked at Sweeny's." Gutierrez pointed to the uniformed cop, laughing in the newsprint photo. "You made this officer look pretty bad. We've gotten some calls, people complaining about a cop laughing at the scene of a murder."

"About that?" It made no sense, but some people didn't have much, Jessie thought. She tried to explain why she'd thought it was a dramatic photo, but he waved the explanation away.

"It's done now," he said. "But I was a little upset, after you'd said the pictures were just for yourself." A *little* upset was an understatement, Jessie decided, looking at his face.

"Well, anyway, what I came about was this picture," she said. To her relief he shut the folder and picked up the print of the backpack. She'd gotten off to a bad start, but maybe they could go on to the important stuff now.

The detective examined the photo carefully for a minute, then dropped it back on the table. "Yeah, we've got some pictures of the bag, Jessie—do you mind if I call you Jessie?" She shook her head, and he went on, his tone more relaxed now. "We also have shots of everything that was in it. Did we miss something important?"

"Well . . ." Jessie pointed at the half-obscured stuffed animal. "I wondered if you'd looked at the Wildcat." She drank some coffee. It was starting to cool, but it was still lousy.

"Number twenty-seven, Art Ducas, junior, free safety," the detective said. "Six three, two hundred twenty pounds. All-American the past two seasons. Looks hot for the pros. Yeah, you could say I noticed the Wildcat."

Her heart sank. Oh, great. Here she was about to suggest they ask Art some questions, and Gutierrez turns out to be a football fan. Even though she was dating a guy on the team, Jessie had no real interest in football. Art was Val's boyfriend— that was how Jessie thought of him. But from the way the detective had quoted Art's position and background, he was obviously a rabid Wildcat fan.

"Um. Well, I've been going out with Randy Beckman . . ."

"Second string, guard, sophomore. Six two, two

35

twenty-five. He could be good if he went after it a little harder, but he's lazy. Needs to beef up a little more, too." Gutierrez smiled at her. "And now I know he likes photographers." The detective's face lost a little of its fatigue as he spoke about the players.

"And he's number sixty-three," Jessie said, smiling back. The smile faded as she went on. "I've got a little stuffed Wildcat just like that one, with sixty-three on the jersey. Randy gave it to me. All the guys on the team got one at the end of the season." She pointed once more to the photo. "I wondered why Laurie had Art's Wildcat. He's been dating my roommate."

"Oh?" The monosyllable was flat; they were back to the original tone of the conversation. "Did you ask him?"

"Yeah. And—" Jessie hesitated, then plunged in. "He said it wasn't his, but I've never seen any others with those jerseys. He said he didn't even know Laurie, and then someone told me he'd been dating her behind Val's—my roommate's—back. So I wondered if you'd asked him about it." She finished and sat back. Now that she'd said it in such simple terms, it didn't sound like much.

"That's all you had?" He sighed and slumped back in his chair. Idly he picked up the photograph again. "We saw it, of course. We went over every item in the backpack. And I spotted the number. I'm a big-time Wildcats fan." Briefly the smile came back. "You probably guessed that. I read about the special souvenir Wildcats

36

the Alumni Association had made for the team. Hang on a second." He stood up and left the room, returning in a few minutes with a familiar little stuffed animal in his hands. He handed it to Jessie, and she looked at it numbly. "A local company's started selling copies. That one's off my desk."

She handed it back to him. "I'm sorry. I guess I should have figured you'd check something like that out."

"Yes, you should have." Gutierrez raised an eyebrow. "That was all that was bothering you?"

"Yes. I mean, no." Jessie hurried to correct herself. "I was wrong about the Wildcat, but he *was* dating Laurie, and he did lie about it."

"Look, Jessie, I can sympathize with your being upset about his lying to your roommate, but frankly, it's none of our business. There's no law against guys lying to their girlfriends, *or* vice versa, and if there were, we'd never be able to hire enough cops to enforce it." He looked up as the door opened.

"Got a minute, Ramon?" A stranger stuck his head in through the door.

"Be right with you," Gutierrez said. The man nodded and withdrew, shutting the door, as Gutierrez stood up. "I'm going to have to cut this short," he said. "As I started to say, yeah, we did ask Ducas if he knew the victim. He may have lied to your roommate, but he didn't to us. The victim had been pestering him, making a play for him. He said he asked her out one time just to get her off his back. That was it." He opened the door. "I'll take you down, then I've got to get back to work."

They headed back to the elevators. Jessie made one last stab at explaining why the whole thing bothered her. "But someone told me Art was really getting involved with Laurie . . ."

"Either way, we're not interested," Gutierrez said. He pushed the button for the first floor. "He said he wasn't, and that's good enough for me. Thanks for coming in, though."

As the door slid open at the lobby, Jessie said, "Well, anyway, thanks for the coffee."

Detective Gutierrez stayed on the elevator. "No thanks needed," he said. "I know what it tastes like." He smiled as the door slid shut.

Feeling disgruntled, Jessie headed back toward campus. The wind had picked up while she'd been inside, and the cold edge of it bit through her windbreaker. By the time she got back to the apartment late that afternoon, she felt completely bummed out. Her mood didn't improve when the hot-water faucet on the kitchen sink wouldn't shut off. She had to call the landlord, who acted as though it were her fault. The whole day had been a mess.

The meeting with Detective Gutierrez had really been a farce. Jessie had a hunch that Gutierrez would have been more interested in Art as a suspect if he had been Joe Average instead of Joe Jock. *Maybe it would have been better if I'd said Randy told me*, she thought as she started some water for tea. But it wouldn't have been fair to drag him into it. Besides, Gutierrez was right—lying was no crime.

Randy was also right: it wasn't any of Jessie's business. But Val was her roommate, and she felt disloyal not saying anything when she knew that Art had lied.

They'd never rescheduled the double date that had been planned for the night of Laurie's death. Friday Jessie came home from the studio to find Val doing her hair. "I was starting to think you'd gotten lost," she greeted Jessie. "Hurry up and change—the guys'll be here in a little while."

"The guys? What's up?" Jessie looked at the clock as she spoke. "Did I forget about a party or something?"

"I just thought it might be nice if all four of us went out tonight," Val said. She fastened a long dangling earring of coral and jet to her earlobe. "We never did after Laurie—after the last time. And lately it seems like you've been avoiding me."

"I haven't been trying to," Jessie said uncomfortably. She hadn't, but she *had* been ducking Art.

"Anyway, I called them earlier and asked if they wanted to make up for the other night, and they both said yes," Val said, fastening on the other earring. "Art thought we could grab a bite to eat and then decide what we wanted to do. Nothing fancy, but you *might* want to get dressed before they get here." She looked at the clock pointedly. Jessie took the hint and went in to shower.

Randy must have told Art by now that Jessie knew about his dating Laurie. Which meant that all of them would know—except Val. But Jessie couldn't think of anything else to do, unless she broke her almost-promise to Randy and told her roommate that Art was a lying sneak. Oh, damn. As Jessie finished dressing, she decided the evening would be a disaster. And she couldn't think of a way to get out of it that wouldn't make things worse.

Art arrived first. If Randy had told him Jessie knew about Laurie, the knowledge didn't seem to bother him. He pulled Val in for a lingering kiss, then sat down on the couch, his legs sprawled out to take up what seemed like half the tiny living room. Val sat in his lap, and he nuzzled her neck as he spoke.

"Didja find that stuff?" he asked.

"Some of it," Val answered. She got up and went into her room, coming back out with her hands full. Art had a habit of leaving things in their apartment. "Here, sweetheart. I couldn't find your hunting knife." She dumped sunglasses, books, and a baseball cap in his lap. He picked up one of the books.

"Good, this is the one the library's been bugging me about. Keep an eye out for that knife, though; I'd hate to lose it. Don't let me forget this junk." He pushed it all onto the floor as Val sat back down.

Randy was twenty minutes late, but when he got there, they decided to take both cars. Art wasn't about to ride in someone else's car when he could be driving his cherry Mustang, and Randy didn't like riding in the cramped backseat of the convertible. They met at a small Italian restaurant not far from campus, and everyone ordered. The food was good, and the portions were large enough to satisfy even the appetites of football players.

"If you ate like that more often, Coach wouldn't be on your tail so much about putting on weight," Art observed as Randy sopped up the last of the sauce on his plate with a piece of garlic bread. Jessie was always amazed at the amount of food the guys could put away. They'd both had a full salad and an extra order of garlic bread with their dinner. She hadn't been able to finish even half of her own order of spaghetti.

Randy grinned around the mouthful. Swallowing, he said, "I worked up an appetite in the weight room this afternoon." He wiped his mouth and went on. "The season's over, and I'm not going to worry about it. When I want to eat, I'll eat, and I'll either gain or I won't." As big as Randy was, the coach had spent most of the season encouraging him to gain more weight.

Val stood up. "I'll be right back. Could someone get me a dish of ice cream? A small one, not a football-player one." She grinned and headed for the ladies' room.

"Sounds good to me," Randy said. He looked around. The only waitress visible was on the other side of the room, taking the order for a large and noisy table, but there was an ice-cream machine by the salad bar. "I guess it's serve yourself. Jessie, you want any?"

"Sure," Jessie said with a smile "Thanks." As he crossed the room, Jessie's heart sank. So far, the foursome had gotten along smoothly, but she hadn't spoken with Art at all. Now they were alone at the table. As soon as Randy was out of earshot, Art spoke.

"Randy said he told you about Laurie." He shot a hard glance at her. "You said anything to Val about it?"

Jessie shook her head. "Not yet. But I wish you'd tell her yourself. It's not fair to lie to her like that."

"Don't give me that crap about it not being *fair*," Art said. "So I dated Laurie once or twice. What Val doesn't know won't hurt her, and it's over now."

"Yeah. Laurie's dead, so it's over."

"Whatever. The point is, you just keep your mouth shut about my business if you know what's good for you." There was a rough edge to his voice that Jessie had never heard before.

"Don't you think it might be Val's business as well?" Jessie demanded. She ignored the threat of Art's last words.

"Not if I don't want to tell her, it isn't," Art said. He scowled at her. "I mean it, Jessie, you keep your mouth shut, or you're going to regret it. If I want to tell Val, I will, and if I don't, nobody else had better." He shut his mouth on the last word as Randy returned to the table with a trayload of ice cream. A moment later Val rejoined them.

"Randy! I said a *small* serving," Val exclaimed.

"That is a small one," Art said. All traces of the snarl that had been on his face a few moments before had vanished in a genial grin.

Randy passed a dish to Jessie, filled with ice cream and two toppings. "I figured Art could finish any you didn't want," he told Val. Then he grinned slyly at Jessie. "I'll help if that's too much for you, Jessie."

"Sure, act innocent," she responded. She had to force herself to sound casual. "You just wanted extra for yourself." She looked at the dish in front of her and made a face. At the moment, the sundae didn't even look appetizing.

By the time the guys finished the last of the ice cream, Jessie had calmed down. She was furious at Art, but she wasn't going to take it out on Val, or on Randy. His threats had backfired. Jessie had made up her mind—she was going to tell Val the truth about Laurie. But not now.

"Where to?" Randy asked. The waitress put the bill facedown on the table, and he picked it up and looked at it. Wincing, he added, "Better be someplace cheap." He fumbled for his wallet.

"Nah, I'll get it," Art said. Art had a kind of "job," working for the company of a local Wildcats fan, but it didn't matter if he showed up for it or not.

Val suggested a movie, mentioning one she wanted to see. That gave Jessie the excuse she'd been hoping for.

"It's great, but I've seen it already," she said. "Why

43

don't the two of you go on? We've got both cars."

"Sweetheart, do you want to?" Val asked Art. He was in an agreeable mood, as though the scene with Jessie had never happened. At his nod Val said, "All right, guess I'll see you back at the apartment, Jessie. Have fun!" The two of them left, and Jessie heaved a sigh of relief.

"I'm surprised you didn't want to go with them," Randy said as they walked back to his Toyota. "You liked that movie. Or did you just want to get me alone?" He grinned at her, his face lit by the interior light as he opened the car door.

"That's not a bad idea," she said, grinning back. As he started the car, she added, "But no, that wasn't the reason. I just didn't want to be around Art any longer."

"He said something while I was getting the sundaes, didn't he? I could tell something was up. You looked mad enough to melt the ice cream by looking at it. But you didn't say anything, so . . ." He pulled away from the curb and let the sentence trail off to nothing.

"I didn't want to spoil your evening. Or Val's." Jessie repeated the brief conversation to him, complete with Art's threats. Randy's hands tightened on the steering wheel, and he bit down on an obscenity.

"That jerk! I'm going to have a talk with him about this." Randy's large hands flexed as he spoke, and Jessie thought he had something more direct than words in mind.

"Don't waste time on it," she said. "I'm going to tell

44

Val her boyfriend's a bully and a liar. He won't do anything to me. I'm almost more afraid of what she'll say, to be honest with you. She's not going to like it."

Randy had picked up too much speed. Now he slowed down and said, "Art's still going to hear about this, believe me. But I'm not sure you should tell Val. She's just going to get hurt."

"Art will hurt her anyway," Jessie said. "This will hurt less. I hope. But she needs to know, for her own protection."

"Hey, you know how Art is—" Randy began.

"Yeah, I know. And I'm pretty tired of it!"

"He's used to playing the field." Randy sounded defensive. "And I don't just mean the football field. If you ask me, Val's asking to get hurt, and she has been all year. She acts like they've already sent out the wedding invitations, and I know damned well Art isn't planning that far ahead. I'm not saying Art should have lied to her, but she's asking for grief."

"She's not asking for this sort of hurt!" Jessie snapped.

"What do you mean?"

"I'm not talking about having her heart broken," Jessie said. She shivered as she remembered the expression on Art's face when he'd threatened her. "I'm talking about hurt, *real* hurt. Physical hurt. I think Art's capable of it if he gets mad enough. And I don't want to see that happen."

She wondered if Art had ever gotten mad at Laurie.

45

4

On Saturdays Jessie normally slept late, but the next morning she was up and dressed early. The state legislature was having one of its periodic battles with the university over money, and a number of classes and programs were threatened with funding cuts. Several student organizations had banded together and organized a protest. Jessie wanted to take part in it because a number of classes in the photography department were in danger. The Center for Creative Photography had reduced hours after the last budget cuts. The center had been one of the lures that had drawn her to the U of A. She was outraged at the prospect of its being limited even more.

As she pulled on her jacket, Val came into the kitchen, yawning. "What are you doing up?" she asked. "It's Saturday, did you forget?"

"The rally. I told you about it a few days ago."

"Oh." Val yawned again. "I'm not going. They'll have enough people there, and it's not like they're going to cut the business programs."

"No, but they're going to cut a lot of other things," Jessie said. She picked up her camera case. "Randy said they're even talking about cutting the athletic department's budget."

"Art said something about that, but I'll believe it when I see it," Val said as she poured the last of the coffee for herself. "The team makes a lot of money for the university."

"Maybe they won't cut football, but there are other sports," Jessie said. "The team's going to be there to support the department, and Randy and I are going out afterward."

"Have a good time." Val sat down at the kitchen table with her coffee and picked up the newspaper. "I'm going to stay here where it's warm." As Jessie left, she noticed the pile of Art's junk still on the living-room floor. He hadn't remembered to take it with him the night before.

When Jessie reached campus, she plunged into the crowd gathered in front of the administration building. Before long she had taken off her jacket and tied it around her waist by the sleeves. It might be winter, but this was still Arizona. It would probably hit seventy degrees by midafternoon.

The rally had drawn a noisy, enthusiastic crowd,

48

spilling across the closed street to the mall. All the Tucson television stations had news crews there. Jessie took her camera out and climbed up on a low brick housing for plumbing that was perfectly positioned for taking pictures. What the speakers were saying was interesting, but Jessie was more interested in the crowd. Here a couple, locked in an embrace, there some boys, skateboarding and ignoring all the activity except when the crowd eddied into their path. Faces. Jessie always liked to photograph faces, their features registering varied expressions and life histories. Through her telephoto lens, she spotted some of her neighbors from the apartment complex, including the cowboys from next door with the loud music.

The various teams were huddled together in a block near the administration building, and they roared as the coaches took turns talking about the need to maintain a balanced sports department. The crowd was excited, and Jessie grinned as a rhythmic chant of "Cats! Cats! Cats!" started. She yelled along with everyone else, but she managed to hold her camera steady. There was Randy. She stopped chanting for a moment as she squeezed the shutter release.

The lens turned her camera into an excellent telescope. She panned the section of the crowd where all the athletes were grouped, taking pictures at intervals. Malcolm, Jaime—there was Randy again, talking with "Rosie" Lewis, the star senior fullback—Kevin, Willie— there was Art . . .

Jessie stopped her slow pan and lowered her camera for a moment. Even from this distance, there was no mistaking that short, determined blonde. But they were too far away for Jessie to see their expressions without the camera. Brenda and Art were paying no attention to the crowd or to the speakers. Brenda's mouth was moving, but with all the noise, Jessie wouldn't have been able to hear her if they'd been five feet away. As she finished speaking, Art's face twisted into an ugly grimace of rage, like the one Jessie had seen the night before. He seemed to be snarling something at Brenda. His words awakened an equal rage in her face. Jessie started snapping pictures. Whatever they were talking about, the expression on Art's face was worth photographing.

Brenda better watch out, Jessie thought as she pressed the shutter release again, then advanced the film for another shot.

The rally broke up after another hour. Jessie didn't try to find Randy in the crush of people. She was visible where she was; let him find her instead. He did, easily.

He groaned when she held up her camera case, but he took her to the studio. Jessie had a key, and Mr. Sweeny had told her she could develop her pictures there anytime. She and Randy talked while she worked. She was fast, already adept at processing film. After the film had dried, Jessie printed a contact sheet, a single sheet with all the exposures on it. She could look at the contact sheet and decide what pictures she wanted to print full-sized.

"Like your new portrait?" She handed Randy the magnifying loupe and pointed at one exposure. The shot was one of several she'd taken of him, and it showed him laughing with Rosie. She cracked up at the expression on his face as he peered at the tiny print. Together, the two football players were more than four hundred pounds of muscle and energy, but in the photo they looked like a pair of mischievous second-grade boys, giggling on the playground. "What's the matter, you don't like it?"

"Just don't let any of the other teams see that." He grinned. "We're supposed to scare them on the field, not crack them up."

She paused. "Well, here's one that should frighten them." Of all the shots she'd taken of Art's argument with Brenda, this one captured his expression best. She pointed to the shot.

"I've seen Art like that on the field," Randy said, handing the magnifying loupe back to her after he'd examined the picture. "Usually late in the game, when we're behind. Means he's ready to tear a receiver's head off. Good picture, Jessie."

"That was how he looked last night at the restaurant," she said quietly. "And he was fighting with Brenda today when I took that."

Randy let out a whistle. "Art had better watch it,"

he said. "Off the field, that's definitely uncool."

"Well, I sure don't want to have him looking at *me* that way again." She resumed her work, making full-size prints from some of the negatives.

Sorting through the photos that evening, Jessie hesitated, then pulled the pictures of Art and Brenda out and put them in a separate envelope. The glassine envelope with the negatives and contact sheet went into the box she called her "work file," which she kept under a table in the apartment. She kept meaning to get everything in it organized and labeled, as Mr. Sweeny recommended, but somehow she never found enough time. Val was on the phone, and a moment's listening told Jessie who was on the other end.

". . . but, sweetheart, I thought we were going up Mount Lemmon tomorrow," Val said. Jessie gritted her teeth. Why Val always got that little-girl whine in her voice when she was arguing with Art was beyond her. It made Val sound ridiculous.

"All right . . . yes . . . I guess that'll have to do . . . love you too. Bye." Val hung up the phone, looking dissatisfied.

"Problems?"

"I thought we were going out tomorrow," Val said, "but Art has to finish a paper. I don't know why he's bothering."

Since he usually doesn't, Jessie finished mentally. It must be nice to have professors who didn't care if you showed up or not. Aloud she said, "Speaking of Art, there's something I have to tell you." Jessie had worried about what to say, but the words came out easily, starting with Art's lie that he hadn't known Laurie, and what Brenda had told her. Jessie wound up by repeating Art's threats to her the night before, and describing his fight with Brenda, pulling out the pictures she'd taken that morning. She finished in less time than she'd expected.

After the first couple of sentences, Val sat rigid, her face frozen. She was furious, but Jessie didn't know if it was at her or at Art. Val didn't leave her wondering for long.

"And you just couldn't wait to tell me, could you," Val said, her voice bitter. "I've been putting up with this since last year. Half the women on this campus are trying to pry Art away from me."

That was more than an exaggeration, but Jessie kept quiet. Val went on, her voice rising. "And the ones who can't get at Art one way, the ones he'd never be interested in, are so jealous they can't stand it. It's like they can't bear to see me with Art because it means they can't have him." Val stopped, breathing hard. "Why do you think I stopped rooming with Brenda? From the first time she met Art, she was after him. When she saw he wasn't interested in her, she started making up lies about him, trying to cause trouble, like that crap about steroids. She's just jealous, and you're acting the same way!"

"I'm not interested in Art," Jessie said, keeping her

voice steady. "I just thought you should know he's been lying to you." She pointed to the photo once more. "I don't know if Brenda's telling the truth about the steroids or not, but you'd better watch out for that temper of his."

"*Sure* you aren't interested in Art," Val said, sarcasm dripping from her voice. "So you've got Randy, big deal. Nice, second-string Randy, who'll never get near the pros, who just wants to be some sort of science nerd . . ."

"Why should Randy care about pro football?" Jessie's temper snapped. "And why the hell should I care about it? At least Randy's willing to use his brains. Plant physiology's a tough field."

"I'm sorry." For a moment the anger in Val's voice faded. "I like Randy, you know that." Her expression and voice both hardened. "But Art is *mine*! And I'm not going to listen to any more lies about him!" She got up and left the room, slamming the bedroom door behind her.

Val didn't speak to Jessie for the rest of the evening, and there was no thaw noticeable in the morning. By lunchtime Jessie had had enough. She hadn't done anything to deserve the deep-freeze treatment. The thump of music coming through the wall from the next apartment was the final straw. She got her bike and headed for campus.

The library was quiet, with fewer students around

than on a school day. Jessie's temper faded as she worked. After all, she'd be pretty upset if she caught Randy cheating. Not that she had any chains on him—she didn't. And there were none on her. But if she decided to date some other guy, she'd at least *tell* Randy, and she'd expect the same treatment in return. That was only fair.

Jessie took a break from her studies and headed for the vending-machine area just outside the main entrance of the library. Sipping at a paper cup of phony "hot cocoa," she reflected that as bad as it was, it at least tasted better than the vending-machine coffee. *Although even that's better than what the detective gave me*, she thought, sitting down at one of the tables. She wondered if it was intentional: make the cops drink lousy coffee, and they'd be rougher on the crooks?

Crooks and killers. Inevitably her thoughts returned to Laurie, which led back to the image of Art's face in her mind, twisted in fury. Lose his temper and beat someone up—Jessie had no doubt he was capable of that. But it was hard to believe he could kill someone deliberately.

She finished her cocoa and started to gather her books when a figure loomed beside her. Art. And from the expression on his face, he'd spoken with Val. It looked as if Jessie was about to find out just how dangerous he was. If she'd thought he looked mad at the rally, she'd been wrong. This time, he was *mad*.

He slapped at the stack of books and knocked them

out of her hands. "Sit down! You're not going anyplace just yet. I need to have a little talk with you." As Jessie fumbled for her books, she looked around, hoping someone else was nearby. But the area was completely deserted.

"Hi, Art," she said, faking nonchalance. "Val said you had a paper to do."

"What the hell did you tell her?" he demanded abruptly.

"The truth," Jessie replied. She kept her voice under control. "That you knew Laurie and you dated her. And that you lied to her about it, although Val could have figured that out for herself."

"Why?" Art's teeth were clenched so tightly, the word barely got out.

"Why did you lie? I don't know, you'll have to answer that yourself." Jessie looked up at him defiantly. "Why did I tell her? I figured she had a right to know."

"I told you to keep your mouth shut," he snarled.

"I know you did," Jessie said. Her voice sounded a lot more confident than she felt, and she hoped her face looked just as confident. "You threatened me. I don't take threats, Art. That was why I decided to tell Val. I wouldn't have if you hadn't tried to scare me."

"It was none of your damned business!"

"As far as I'm concerned, it was," Jessie said. "You were hurting my roommate by lying to her, and you were threatening me. That made it my business. Oh, and I told Val about your fight with Brenda, too.

56

What was that all about, Art? Did you try to bully her the way you did me?"

"She's another damned troublemaker, like you," Art said. "She'd better stop blabbing that mouth of hers . . ."

"Or what, Art?"

"You're the one who hurt Val," Art said, changing the subject abruptly. He seemed to be getting madder as he spoke, as though he was working himself up. "By talking. What I tell her is my business, not yours. And anything I say to you is my business and not Val's."

"It's her business if it's threats," Jessie said. "She has a right to know you're the sort who uses them. And I don't have to put up with them. Art, get this straight." Jessie stood up, facing him. He was a head taller than she was, and over a hundred pounds heavier, but she gave him back glare for glare. "Every time you threaten me, I'm going to tell Val. And Randy. You'd better be ready to back your threats up, because I'm not going to keep quiet about them."

"I'll back them up," he growled, blood rushing to his face. His hands had clenched into fists. "I'll . . ."

"Excuse me." Jessie hadn't seen the older woman approaching. "The machine's out of order. Do you have change for a dollar?" The woman gave no indication she noticed anything wrong, though Art looked as if he were about to have a stroke. He turned his back and moved away a few steps, fists clenched at his

57

sides. Jessie fumbled in her purse, finding some quarters and enough small change to make up a dollar. Her hands were shaking and she dropped a dime. She and the woman both stooped to pick it up.

"Is he bothering you?" the woman whispered.

Jessie nodded, not trusting herself to speak.

"Shall I call the police?"

"No," Jessie whispered back, finding her voice. "Just walk back to the library with me." The woman nodded, and they both stood up.

As the woman went over to the machines, Art came back over to Jessie. "Who's that old bat?" he growled.

"I have no idea," Jessie replied truthfully. "But I meant what I said, Art. I'll do you one last favor. I won't tell Val about this unless you try threatening me again." The woman was coming back from the machines now, and Jessie picked up the stack of books Art had knocked out of her hands earlier.

"Dammit, Jessie, you listen to me. . . ." Art's angry mutter was cut off as the woman stopped beside them.

"See you around, Art," Jessie said. Her attempt at a casual tone failed, but it was close enough. She and the woman went into the library, leaving Art standing there alone.

"Thanks," Jessie said, as soon as the door swung shut. "That was pretty awkward."

"It looked worse than that," the woman said crisply. "Are you sure you don't want to call the police?"

Jessie shook her head.

"Well, then, just remember you don't have to put up with that sort of nonsense." Jessie smiled faintly at this echo of her own words. "I'll be here for a few hours, if you change your mind and need a witness. Down in the microfilm room." The woman left, heading for the elevator.

Jessie could see Art outside the plate-glass windows along the front of the library. He was half-hidden by one of the concrete pillars that supported the overhanging upper stories of the building, but even in the shadows the expression on his face was obvious. He scowled at her, and she turned back into the library, thankful for the bright lights and the people moving around the card catalogs. Art might be angry, but he wouldn't come in here and make a scene.

She went up to the next floor and made her way to the far end of the stacks, finding a chair near a window. After a while she saw a familiar red convertible driving away. Jessie felt ashamed. For all her brave words, she'd run away from him.

For a long time Jessie sat there thinking. The more she saw of Art's temper, the more dangerous she thought he was. Maybe he *was* using steroids. From what she'd read about them, violent temper was a pretty common side effect of the drugs. Whether his temper was natural or from a pill, though, it scared her. The question was, Was he a danger to Val? Or to Jessie herself?

Jessie was up early the next morning. Her design

class was meeting for a special session. The instructor had planned several of these sessions to capture the distinctive lighting effects of different times of the day and year. Jessie bundled up; the forecast the night before had been for heavy frost. She hoped it would warm up fast.

She grabbed her camera and backpack and headed out the door just as the sun cleared the roofs and the first watery rays of winter sunlight hit the front window of the apartment. As she pulled the door quietly closed behind her, she heard Val's radio alarm come on in the middle of a song. Seven thirty. Jessie was running late; she'd have to hurry.

She was halfway to the street when she saw the blood.

60

5

A small puddle ran out from under the pyracantha bushes and spilled over the edge of the sidewalk. Jessie stopped, straddling her bike. The bright red, already fading to brown where it had dried around the edges, was unmistakable. She looked down the sidewalk. An irregular line of small brownish dots, vivid against the light cement, trailed into the street. They looked as if they'd come from an oil leak. Jessie fought a rising sickness at the back of her throat, knowing the substance was a more vital fluid than that.

She dropped her bike. The bushes were thick, almost waist high, but she could see a shape beneath them. She pushed branches aside, forcing her way through until she was bent double over a figure in a red-and-white jogging outfit. Brenda. There were drops of blood like beads on the leaves and ground. Jessie

gagged as she realized the jogging outfit was all white—
the red on it was blood. She reached for Brenda's hand.
It was limp and ice-cold, cold in a way no living flesh
could be. For a moment Jessie held it, her fingers grop-
ing for a pulse in the icy wrist. It was like handling rubber, a doll, a *thing*. Jessie let go, and the arm flopped
loosely back. It didn't fall all the way to the ground, getting tangled in some branches. There were berries on
the branches. Tiny red berries that looked like drops of
blood.

Jessie straightened up and looked around un-
steadily. No one was in sight. She was alone. Except
for—she looked back at the clump of bushes. Brenda
was there, but she was dead. Jessie felt hollow, and
more terrified than she'd ever been in her life. She had
a feeling that she shouldn't leave the body alone.
Jessie could only think of one way to get help without
leaving Brenda.

Very deliberately she began to scream and scream.

Her screams had brought people running. Within a
few minutes the first squad car had arrived, followed
shortly by an ambulance and the first of the detectives. Now she stood shivering, watching as the same
efficient people she'd seen two weeks before moved
around performing the same mysterious duties. She
sipped at the mug of tea she held, savoring its warmth.
One of the neighbors had handed her the mug, and
she hadn't even noticed who it was.

It wasn't the temperature that was making her feel so chilled; it was the memory of Brenda's icy hand. The tea made a tiny center of warmth in her stomach, but it didn't touch the deeper cold Jessie felt. It had been hard to stop screaming once help had arrived, as though her nerves had demanded the release. But she had finally regained her self-control. If only she could stop shivering.

The police tape extended down the street in front of the apartment complex, following the drops of blood. The medics were bent over the body, which was now lying on a stretcher on the sidewalk. She had *known* Brenda was dead as soon as she touched that hand. No, as soon as she'd seen her. But she supposed they had to try, no matter how pointless it seemed.

The residents of the complex were milling around, staying behind the tape but watching curiously as more cars pulled up. Val was talking to the guys from the next apartment. Jessie hadn't met them before; she'd just seen them in passing and in the laundry room. Now Val introduced them as though this were a party. She was dressed only in her robe, with a towel around her head; she'd been in the shower when Jessie had started screaming. After a few more minutes, she headed inside the apartment to get dressed. The shorter of the two guys asked Jessie something, but she wasn't listening. After a moment he walked away to talk to the manager of the complex. She wasn't even sure what his name was. Paul, Pat—it wasn't important.

She went back to watching the activity around Brenda.

A TV news van pulled up, and a man got out with a camera. Other photographers and cameramen were as close to the now-sheeted figure of Brenda as possible. Cameras. Jessie hadn't taken any photos. It didn't feel right. Besides, she had an official position in the drama. She was the one who had discovered the body. But she couldn't stop taking pictures in her mind: freeze-frame shots of the police, the medics, the ambulance.

Another car parked just outside the taped-off area, and a familiar figure got out. Gutierrez. *Of course*, Jessie thought, *he handled Laurie's murder. He'd be called in for this one as well*. With a start Jessie realized what she was thinking. Art's arguments with Brenda, the vicious look on his face in those pictures—without realizing it, she'd come to the conclusion that Art had murdered Brenda. And he must have been the one who'd killed Laurie.

She glanced back toward the door of her own apartment. Poor Val. It was going to be rough when she found out, but at least she was alive. Somehow Jessie didn't think being Art Ducas's girlfriend was compatible with a high life expectancy. Gutierrez spoke with one of the cops in uniform, then made his way toward Jessie. As he neared, there was a flash of recognition in his face, and a look as though he'd bitten into something sour. It vanished almost at once, leaving the smooth, professional blankness Jessie had seen before.

"I hadn't expected to see you again, Jessie," he said. He glanced around. "Do you get mixed up in this sort of thing often?" He gestured vaguely at the activity behind them.

"Mixed up in?" she repeated blankly. That wasn't how she'd thought of it.

Nor, apparently, was it the way he really saw things, as he added hastily, "Just a little joke, sorry. But it's rather unusual to have a witness show up at two unrelated murders within a matter of days." He cocked his head slightly to one side, looking at her to see how she took this.

"Unrelated? But I thought . . ." Jessie broke off, confused. She suddenly realized the police had no reason to assume the two killings were connected. They hadn't seen what she had, the fights and Art's temper.

"You thought what?" Gutierrez prompted her.

"I just thought, since you were here, I mean *you* being here, not just the police, I thought . . ." Her sentence was getting hopelessly tangled, and Jessie took a deep breath and started over. "I figured the police must believe the two killings are related, since they put the same guy in charge."

He shook his head. "So far, the only connection I'm aware of is you. Did you know this girl as well?"

"Her name's Brenda Wolinsky," Jessie said. Her heart sank. At the moment, *she* looked more suspicious than Art. It was a good thing she'd been at the studio when Laurie had been run over. "She's a student, she used to live here."

"Here?" He looked around the apartment building.

Jessie nodded. "She used to live with my roommate. She moved out and I moved in just before Thanksgiving."

"Let's get some details." The notebook was out, and Jessie started answering the detective's questions. When she had answered as many as she could, she asked one of her own.

"If the police don't think this murder's got anything to do with Laurie's murder, why *did* they send the same detective?"

"It's not officially a murder yet," Gutierrez said. "Although I think we can rule out suicide, and no one gets stabbed that many times by accident."

"How many—I mean, can you already tell how she . . ." Jessie couldn't finish the question.

"How she died." He scowled. "She died right there behind those bushes, looks like. Whoever it was didn't know what he was doing, from the number of times she was stabbed. It's too bad someone didn't come along while she was lying there—we might have saved her. She lay there and bled to death."

Jessie's stomach tightened into a hard ball, and she felt sick. She'd been in her apartment, Brenda's old one, getting up, getting ready for another day while Brenda had been there in the bushes less than fifty yards away, dying.

66

"The medics tried, but it was too late," Jessie said.

Gutierrez snorted. "Hell, they knew it was too late when they started. Medics are just three or four more people to walk all over the evidence." He hastily added, "They've got a job to do, and sometimes they can do some good. But it's hard on us when they move the body around and mess up the scene."

"But they had to see if they could save her life," Jessie said, then stopped as he shook his head.

"She was already dead," he said. "Couldn't you tell that when you found her?"

Jessie said nothing, remembering the feel of Brenda's hand. She'd known, all right.

The murder weapon had turned up in the same pyracantha bushes that had hidden the body. It was a cheap-looking stainless-steel knife with a metal handle. "Easy to clean, impossible to trace," Detective Gutierrez had explained. The police photographer took pictures of it, while everyone pressed as close as they could to watch. That was one of the few recognizable items that turned up, from Jessie's inexpert view. Various things were marked and photographed that meant nothing to her, but it was obvious they meant a lot to the cops.

The evidence Jessie had was less mysterious, to her way of thinking: an eyewitness account of a fight between Art and Brenda, corroborated by photographs.

No matter how big a football fan the detective was, he'd eventually have to investigate this fight.

Over four hours had passed since Jessie had found Brenda. The body had been taken away in the same unmarked van that had transported Laurie. Now it seemed as though the police were finishing up. The various small items that had been photographed earlier were put into plastic bags, including the knife. Jessie leaned her head back against the rough bricks of the apartment building for a moment. It felt as though she'd lived through a couple of centuries since she'd gotten up that morning. The thought passed through her mind that she'd missed her class. She wondered if finding a body would count for an excused absence.

She opened her eyes as a familiar voice spoke beside her. "Jessie? I'd like to go over just a few more things with you." It was Gutierrez, back again as promised.

"All right," Jessie said, straightening up. "Can we go up to my apartment? I've got something I want to show you, and I'd like to sit down for a while."

"Sure. You didn't have to stay outside all this time." He followed her back to the apartment.

The door was unlocked, but Val wasn't there. Jessie had a vague memory of her roommate saying she was going someplace, but she couldn't remember where. The coffee maker was still on, and there was half a pot left. Val's absence made things a lot easier for Jessie.

"Want some?" she asked the detective, pouring herself a cup. She needed the jolt from the caffeine, as well as another few minutes, before trying to explain her suspicions and why she'd taken photos of Art and Brenda.

"Sure." He accepted the cup and added cream. Taking a sip, he smiled slightly. "Better than what we served you. Thanks. Now"—he settled back into a chair at the kitchen table—"just what did you have to tell me?" He waited, face impassive but notebook ready.

"I think I know who did it," she said. She took a deep breath, then continued in a rush. "Art Ducas. Remember I told you he was dating Laurie? Well, it was more than just one or two dates, and he lied about it, and then he fought with Brenda over it. She was the one who told me about Art and Laurie. And he called her a troublemaker"—the thought passed through her mind, *Just as he did me*, but she didn't repeat it out loud—"and then he had an argument with her. He's got a mean temper."

"He's a football player," Gutierrez said. He set his cup down on the table and looked at Jessie with a completely neutral expression. "Football players aren't usually famous for saintly tempers. Have you got any proof of this fight, besides the word of a dead girl? And why would he kill her? Just temper?"

"He was mad because she was telling people about him and Laurie," Jessie said. "That's the first link— Laurie. But I've got proof of the fight. I took photos. I'll go get them."

69

"Can't have been much of a fight if they let you take pictures," the detective muttered. "I told you before, we're satisfied with Ducas's story."

Sure, Jessie thought, *because you don't want to admit that a big star player could be mixed up in this.* She started looking through the papers on the coffee table; she was sure she'd left the envelope with the photos there. While she searched, she repeated everything Brenda had told her. Ironically, Brenda's death had convinced Jessie it was all true. But Brenda hadn't offered any proof about the steroids.

Proof. Where were those pictures? She went back through the stack of papers, some of them spilling to the floor as her search became more frantic. Gutierrez watched her impassively.

"They're around here somewhere," she said, half under her breath. Raising her voice, she added, "I'll find them in just a minute. It was a real fight." She got her work file from under the table and upended it on the floor while she described the fight, Art's threats at the restaurant, the scene at the library. But she couldn't find the pictures, and quietly Gutierrez cast doubt on each point she brought up, one by one.

She hadn't heard what Art and Brenda were fighting about.

No one had noticed anything at the restaurant.

She didn't know the name of the woman at the library.

Art had never tested positive for steroid use in the past.

And she still couldn't find the pictures.

Jessie's heart sank with each of Gutierrez's calm rejoinders. She knew she wasn't imagining the menace Art had projected, but the possibility of his guilt melted away as the detective dismissed each of her arguments. He wanted cold, hard facts, fingerprints, things he could examine or put under a microscope.

Or the pictures. The envelope with the negatives from the rally wasn't in the box either. Jessie straightened up and realized it was no use. She'd trashed the place searching. The pictures probably would never be seen again. Of course they were gone, she thought. Art had been there yesterday.

"All right," she said, sinking onto the couch. She felt tired. "I can't find the photos. But they did have a fight, and Art did threaten me. He scared the hell out of me, if you want to know the truth." She looked up at Gutierrez challengingly. "Do you think I'm lying?"

"I think you're exaggerating," the detective answered calmly. "It happens a lot, we're used to it. Most people who find themselves caught up in the edges of a crime tend to enlarge their own role, figure they have important clues when it's a handful of nothing. I'm not saying that's the case here—"

"It sure sounds like you are," Jessie said bitterly.

"It could be. It could be jealousy, as well." At that, Jessie's mouth dropped open. He nodded, as though she'd said something, and went on. "Oh, yeah, that happens. There are a few nut cases around who call up on every homicide in the city, accusing the mayor or their garbageman or their brother-in-law. You'd be surprised how often the motivation for that sort of thing is jealousy. Or a relationship gone sour."

"That's ridiculous, I don't even like Art," Jessie said.

"So I gathered," Gutierrez said. "Which is part of why I think you're exaggerating. That doesn't mean you can't be jealous."

Jessie took a deep breath, but before she could say anything, the front door banged open and Val came in. "Jessie! Have you heard any more . . ." Val's voice trailed off as she spotted the stranger. Gutierrez got to his feet as she did.

"Val, this is Detective Gutierrez," Jessie told her.

"I understand you used to live with the dead girl," he said. "I wonder if I could ask you a few questions." He gestured to his still-open notebook.

"Sure, I guess so," Val said. She looked at Jessie uncertainly. "Will it take long? I've got some wash in the laundry room."

"Not too long," he said. Jessie doubted that. "I'd like to speak with you in private, if you don't mind."

Jessie stood up. "Val, you want me to go get your stuff?"

"Would you?" Val asked. "Thanks, it's in the dryer."

"Thanks for your help, Jessie," Gutierrez added. He was polite, but he was telling her to leave.

The laundry room was warm and noisy, filled with the smell of clean fabric and laundry products. Jessie sat on top of the dryer and wondered if, back in the apartment, the detective was telling Val about her theories. She hoped not, and she didn't really think so: she was quite sure the cop hadn't been interested in her theories. Instead, he seemed to think Jessie was just another nut case. At best, he thought she was imagining things. Was she, she wondered?

Art, knocking the books from her hands. She shook her head. She hadn't imagined that. She hadn't imagined the look of hatred twisting his handsome face. And she hadn't imagined the pictures.

Or the fact that they were missing.

Gutierrez had left by the time Jessie got back to the apartment. She was relieved to find out that he hadn't mentioned her at all. According to Val, he hadn't said much of anything, just asked questions about the people Brenda had known, and what her habits were.

Val and Jessie barely spoke to each other the rest of the day, each wrapped in her own thoughts. Jessie was tired and depressed. She didn't want to think about that horrible moment when she'd realized what had happened. Val flipped through the television channels, then started hunting through videos, as though searching for escape. Jessie went to bed early. She was

73

exhausted, and sleep would help her put all this behind her.

In the morning she still felt tired. She was scheduled to work that day, and she headed for the studio, planning to look around one last time for the photos. She was sure they weren't there, but it wouldn't hurt to check.

Jack Sweeny was in the darkroom when she arrived, and he immediately put her to work helping him. As they worked, she told him everything that had happened, from spotting the first drops of blood to the talk with Gutierrez.

"Why didn't you take any pictures?" was his first question when she stopped speaking. "You could have compared them with the ones you took the first time. Maybe you could have spotted something unusual."

"I—it didn't seem right," Jessie stammered.

"It should have." She thought she knew this lecture, but today Jack gave it a different twist. "You're developing an eye. Which means that sometimes you'll take a picture and you won't even know why it's important till you look at it later." Jessie thought about the picture of Laurie's backpack, which had started her suspicions, and said nothing. He was right, she realized. There had been something—Jessie suddenly wished she had taken a picture of Brenda, lying in the pyracantha bushes. Something was itching at the edge of her memory, something that hadn't looked right.

"Do you think you're right about that guy?" Jack asked.

Jessie nodded. Despite what Gutierrez had said, she *knew* she hadn't been imagining any of it.

"Then you should have taken pictures," he said. "That camera is your eye—learn to use it."

As he spoke, Jessie felt her resolve harden. No matter what the police thought, Art was involved in this somehow. Jessie thought that Val might be Art's next victim. And since the cops weren't going to do anything to stop him, she would have to.

The question was, What could she do?

Jessie didn't think of an answer until she was leaving English class the next day. As she cut across the lawn toward the student union, she spotted Art talking to a couple of girls. As Jessie watched, he waved a casual farewell to the girls and headed down the mall. For some reason Jessie began to follow him. It just seemed like the natural thing to do.

He's not going to do anything in public, Jessie thought. But he had been openly flirting with those girls, as though he didn't care if anyone saw him.

Over the next few days, Jessie tried to follow Art around campus, hoping to find out if he was actually guilty of committing a crime. The biggest thing she discovered was that shadowing people was a lot harder than books and movies had led her to believe. Several times she found Art staring back at her. The first time, he just looked surprised. But by the third time it happened, he had figured out that she wasn't around just by coincidence. He overtook her on a crowded sidewalk and grabbed her by the arm.

"What the hell do you think you're doing?" he asked.

"Ow!" Jessie cried, jerking her arm loose. "I'm on my way to class, that's all." She kept walking, staring straight ahead, and hoped he hadn't seen her following him earlier in the day.

"You don't have any classes on this side of campus," he said. He stayed alongside her, elbowing others out of his way. "What are you following me around for?"

"I'm not," she said. She walked faster, trying to ignore him, but he kept step easily.

"Quit bugging me, Jessie. I told you that once before." Someone called to him. He grabbed her arm one last time, adding in a low tone, "I'm not going to tell you again." Then he released her and turned. "Hey, Beal!" He headed toward the guy who had called him, and Jessie stood still, rubbing her arm and watching them. Just before they disappeared around the corner, Art glared back at her briefly. She'd have to be more careful.

After four days of following Art, Jessie was discouraged. She couldn't spend her entire life playing detective. She had classes and a job and her own boyfriend. Besides, nothing suspicious had happened. Mr. Sweeny might be right about the camera catching more than the photographer saw, but so far hers hadn't caught anything worth seeing.

She leaned on the low concrete wall of the Cherry Avenue parking garage. She was standing on the second floor, looking down at a side entrance to McKale Center, the sports complex. Art had vanished inside the center a half hour earlier. She was trying to read and watch the door at the same time, and her mind kept wandering from the page. So far, if the police were making any progress finding the murderer, the newspaper wasn't reporting it. The story of Brenda's death had slipped with alarming speed from page one to the second section. Laurie's murder wasn't even mentioned any longer. The same thing would happen with Brenda. The U of A was a big school, and Tucson was a big town. The deaths of two college students weren't even nine-days' wonders. More like three days.

If Art was arrested for the murders, though, that would be national news. Every sports section in the country would cover the story.

Jessie straightened up, slipping her book into her purse. There was Art now. He turned his head, speaking to someone behind him. *Oh, no,* she thought. Randy was with him, his face red and sweaty. They must have been working out in the weight room together.

Jessie stepped back a half pace. The slight movement caught Art's eye; he looked right at Jessie, then

79

yelled. She turned and ran into the depths of the garage—she didn't know what else to do. The low concrete roof made the building an echo chamber, and she stopped, aware of how loud her footsteps were. She heard a shout that sounded like Randy, but the distorted, echoing words were impossible to understand. Great—she was hiding from her own boyfriend. But she couldn't explain to Randy why she'd been following Art. Not with Art listening, anyhow. After fifteen minutes of hiding behind a parked car, she left the garage cautiously. Normal traffic swirled around, cars passed on Cherry Avenue, joggers trotted by, students with backpacks and books headed into the library. Art and Randy were nowhere in sight.

So much for my career as a private detective, Jessie thought glumly. She'd never felt like such a complete jerk in her life. If she had just stayed there and faced them—but she hadn't. She didn't even want to think about what Randy would say.

Jessie was relieved that Randy didn't call that night. Someday she was going to have to learn to *think* before getting herself into these ridiculous situations. She'd always been too impulsive, and it had gotten her into trouble before. Like arguing with Art at the library that day. The incident this afternoon had been silly and embarrassing, but the other one could have been deadly. Those large hands clenching into fists—if that woman hadn't turned up when she did, Art could have pounded Jessie to a pulp.

In the morning she went through the paper twice, but there was nothing at all about Brenda's murder. She picked up the paper from the day before and reread the short article. Jessie hadn't realized Brenda lived nearby. Val had told the police about Brenda's habit of jogging every morning, and they'd discovered her route. The paper had printed a map the day after the murder. The path Brenda ran on led by the apartment building. Val told Jessie that she'd gone along a few times on the same path when Brenda was her roommate, and Art had joined them too. Jessie noted that fact grimly. He would have known where to find Brenda.

The biggest question in Jessie's mind was why Brenda was killed in front of the apartment building. There were two possible explanations: Brenda had threatened to tell Val something, and Art had waited here to stop her; or Art had left Brenda there as a warning to Jessie.

Jessie could hear Art's words again. *"She's another damned troublemaker, like you."*

And now Brenda couldn't make any more trouble for Art.

The next day Jessie went to the student union for a Coke and some fries. As she came out, she halted abruptly in the doorway, standing there until someone behind her nudged her roughly. She moved out of the way, not paying any attention to the other students entering and leaving around her. Art was in front of the building, talking to a girl Jessie had never seen before. As she watched, he put his arm around the girl's waist and they walked away.

Jessie automatically took out her camera and focused before they'd gone fifty feet. She shot a couple of fast pictures, then followed at a careful distance. Since everyone on campus seemed to be on the mall that afternoon, it was easy for Jessie to remain out of Art's sight. Art and the girl cut across the mall as Jessie dodged around a knot of students and ducked behind the memorial fountain. His attention was on his companion; he didn't seem to notice anything else. Including, for once, Jessie.

They went past the fountain and cut in front of the library, Jessie following the whole way. As they crossed Cherry Avenue, she hung back. There weren't as many people here, and she now knew where Art was heading. They disappeared inside the same parking garage Jessie had hidden in the day before. She waited outside, watching, with her camera ready.

A few minutes later the red Mustang roared out and took off down Cherry Avenue. It was warm enough for Art to have the top down, and the girl with him was laughing, her long silky black hair flying in the wind. Jessie took one last picture, then watched until they turned the corner. After zipping her camera case, she turned to go back to the student union, where she'd left her bike. Then she stopped, appalled.

Someone else had seen Art and the brunette. Val stood near the corner, staring in the direction the convertible had gone, with tears streaming down her face.

As soon as she'd spotted Val, Jessie went over to her, figuring she'd need a shoulder to cry on, but Val had stormed off. By the time Jessie got back to the apartment, Val had apparently convinced herself that the girl in the Mustang meant nothing. When Jessie told her she'd followed them from the student union, Val exploded.

"You were *following* him. I think that's disgusting," Val glared at her. "What would you say if I started following your precious Randy around?"

"Val, I think Art knows more than he's saying about these murders," Jessie argued. "And he's got a temper, and he's lied to you, and I don't want to see you get hurt." *Emotionally or otherwise*, she added mentally.

"I'm not going to be. Art wouldn't hurt me, he *loves* me." Val's chin came up defiantly. "I don't care what it looked like this afternoon. He loves me, I know he does. And I love him!"

It was no use talking to her. "Well, I warned you," Jessie said, glancing at the clock. Randy was due to pick her up for a date in half an hour. "Don't ever say I didn't warn you."

"I'm not likely to," Val said. "But for the record, I don't believe you were following Art because you were protecting me. You've been hanging around him so much—I think you'd like to trade Randy for a new model. Well, you can't have Art."

"You're crazy if you think I want him," Jessie said bluntly. "As a matter of fact, I think you're crazy to want him yourself, but it's your—" She almost said "funeral." The word was altogether too appropriate. She completed the sentence. "—choice. Anyway, I have to get ready."

When Jessie came out of her bedroom, Val was sitting curled up on the couch, her face pensive. Jessie didn't try to reopen the conversation; instead she sat there flipping channels on the TV until Randy picked her up. When they left ten minutes later, Val still hadn't said a word.

"Were you two having a fight?" Randy asked as they got into the car.

"We were earlier," Jessie said, fastening her seat belt.

"Were you fighting about Art?" Jessie noticed the constraint in Randy's voice. He'd never sounded so stiff before.

"Yeah, I was trying to warn her about—" Randy stiffened slightly and she broke off. "Randy, what's wrong?"

"You've been following Art around campus," he said coldly. "Why?"

"How did you know?" The memory of her flight

from the parking garage the day before came back to her as she said it.

"I saw you running away yesterday. I asked Art what the hell that was all about, and he told me you've been chasing him. Following him around campus, even cutting classes, getting all dreamy-eyed."

"*What?*"

"Weren't you?" Randy didn't even glance at her; he continued to stare straight ahead.

"*No!* I was—" She ran her hand through her hair. "It's a long story. But it wasn't like that!"

"I have time," Randy said. "I'm listening."

For the next ten minutes he said nothing as Jessie poured out all her suspicions to him. Her biggest concern was Val's safety. Art's temper made him dangerous to be close to. Especially girlfriend-close.

He started with an awkward question. "So you were following him. But why did you run away from *me?*" His eyes remained on the road, but his attention was on her.

"Panic," Jessie said, disgusted with herself. "Pure panic. I didn't want to tell Art what I was doing, especially in front of you." She paused as a fresh thought struck her. "Do you mean to tell me that Art claims I've got the hots for him?"

"More or less," Randy said. "He figured it was the only reason for you to be following him around like that. It's happened before with him."

"So he says," she said dryly. "Sorry, I don't buy it.

Art may think he's God's gift to women, but that doesn't mean women agree with him. I know there are a few who do that sort of thing, but not many."

"A few like Laurie," he said. Jessie fell silent. "Or like Brenda. Actually, I'm not so sure about her. I know she followed Art around for a while, but she may have been playing detective." Randy glanced sideways.

"All right, I earned that. I guess it all sounds silly."

"It sounds worse than that, it sounds unbelievable." Randy cut off her protests. "No, I believe that was why you were doing it." He shifted his right hand from the gearshift to pick up her hand and give it a squeeze. "You don't play games, and I can't see you falling for Art, not really. I just got jealous when I thought you'd—you should have figured what it would look like." He dropped her hand. "But this wild idea that Art's some sort of maniac killer—Jessie, that's impossible!"

"I don't think so," she said stubbornly.

"Look, I've played ball with him." Randy turned onto a main cross street, heading for the foothills. "Sure, he's got a temper—Coach chewed him out for it a million times this season. And sometimes he gets a little carried away off the field; I've seen him. It's ugly, but it doesn't make him a *murderer*!"

"How about the steroids?" Jessie asked.

"I don't believe he's on them," Randy said. "Everybody always says football players are on steroids.

They've said it about me, for God's sake."

"But Art's temper . . ."

"He's always had a temper, far as I know. Not everybody with a temper is doing drugs."

"He's still dangerous," Jessie said quietly.

"Yeah, I know." There was silence for a moment, then Randy spoke again. "He was way out of line trying to lean on you that way, and if he tries it again, he's going to regret it. He knows that. I've warned him." Randy's hands tightened on the steering wheel. "But he's not a murderer. The cops aren't even interested in him."

"Detective Gutierrez did ask Art some questions," Jessie said. "But he's a big Wildcats fan. I'll bet he knows Art's birthday, and how much you weighed as a baby, and what Rosie's class standing was in high school."

"Probably not," Randy said, grinning. "Class rank and birthdays don't matter on the field. He probably could tell you what Rosie's chances are on the draft, though."

"I don't think Gutierrez would cover up anything," Jessie said, returning to the subject. "But I think he's tagged Art in his mind as off-limits. He acted like he thought I was nuts when I tried to tell him about Art's fight with Brenda." *Not just nuts, like I was after Art. Which is what Val thought.*

"I don't know," Randy said. He sounded irritated. "I just don't like the idea of my girlfriend following some other guy around campus all the time." He pulled off the road at a spot where there was a wide gravel shoulder and a terrific view of the city, lights twinkling in the distance. "And I'd just as soon not spend our whole date talking about him, either." They said no more of Art.

Even later in the evening, when they drove slowly back to the apartment, the subject wasn't renewed. There was a reminder of it, though, when they pulled in front of the building. Art's Mustang was parked there.

"Want to come in for a few minutes?" Jessie asked. She glanced at the convertible as she spoke.

"I don't know. Art's there. Hate to break anything up."

"My going in would, anyway," Jessie said quickly. "And—I'd like it. Please." She didn't know how Art would react when he saw her, but she'd feel safer if there was someone else around. Preferably someone as big as Art.

"Well . . ." Randy got out of the car. "But I'm not up for any hassles right now."

"Neither am I," Jessie said. The chill she felt had little to do with the near-freezing air.

They had just reached the door of the apartment when there was a crash and a scream, cut short, from inside the apartment.

"What the . . ." Randy banged the door wide open, and the pair inside froze as though caught by a flashbulb. Val was on the kitchen floor, struggling to get to her feet. Near her one of the chairs lay on its side. It had been stacked high with books, and they had landed everywhere.

Art stood over Val, his hand still raised as though to strike her.

"What the hell do you think you're *doing?*" Randy had taken two long steps forward and grabbed Art's hand, locking his wrist in a grip as tight as handcuffs. "Art! Cut it out, man!" Randy twisted Art's arm a bit, forcing him back toward the living room. Art's free hand came up and shoved back at Randy, but Randy ignored it. Jessie bent over Val.

"I'm—I'm all right," her roommate stammered. Her face had gone a chalky white. "I fell."

"Yeah, right." Val scrambled to her feet, and Jessie hesitantly put an arm around her shoulders. For a moment Val was stiff; then she almost collapsed into Jessie's arms, crying. "Sure. You fell." She patted Val on the back and glared over her shoulder at Art. Randy had turned him loose, and he was now scowling at Jessie and rubbing his wrist. He started to take a step toward Jessie and Val, and Randy stepped in front of him.

"We're going to have a little talk, Art," he said. "Sit down." Art stepped to one side as if to dodge around Randy. "I said, *sit down!*" The last word was a roar as Randy almost threw Art onto the couch. He landed so hard he bounced, and Jessie heard the thin *crack* of breaking wood inside the furniture. Art slumped back against the cushions, all the fight suddenly gone out of him.

"What happened?" Jessie asked. She felt ridiculous asking the question, but they had to start somewhere.

"Nothin'," Art slurred. "Just nothin'. And it's none of your—"

"Shut up, Art," Randy cut him off. "You're too drunk to answer." He glared at Art, who muttered some obscenities but didn't meet his eye.

"I—we had a fight," Val said. She had stopped crying by now and was darting quick, frightened looks back and forth between Art and Randy. "Art had some beers earlier, and I wanted to talk, and he wasn't in the mood." Jessie could guess what Val had wanted to talk about: Art's cheating. He'd never be in the mood to talk about that.

"He hit you?" Randy looked disgusted. "Even drunk, he ought to know better. You want me to call the cops?"

At that, Art sat up a little straighter, and some of the drunken foolishness left his face. "Hey, man, c'mon . . . ," he started. Randy ignored him.

"It's up to you, Val," Randy said. "If you want to file a complaint, Jessie and I are witnesses."

"I—no, Randy, please don't call the police." Val's face had a little color in it now, and she walked over to the couch with a step that was almost steady. "It was just a misunderstanding, that's all." She sat down beside Art without looking at him.

"Misunderstanding? Is that what you call it?" Randy sounded as disgusted as Jessie felt. *I don't believe this*, Jessie thought. *She's going to let him get away with it.*

"I'm sorry," Art said in a low voice. "She's right, I was drunk, but it's cool now. You don't have to call the cops, it won't happen again."

Jessie didn't believe him, but for now the excitement was over. Art stood up with a groan, favoring one leg, and Val fussed over him. From the way she was behaving, anyone would have thought Art was the one who'd been hurt.

Randy came over to Jessie and spoke in a low tone. "He's shook up, but that doesn't mean he's sober. I'm going to drive him home." He glanced back over his shoulder at the others, who were standing in the living room now, their arms around each other. "Think you can talk some sense into Val? She's just setting herself up for more trouble if she lets him get away with this."

"I told you he was dangerous," Jessie whispered.

That brought a sharp look from Randy, but no other response.

He managed to convince Art to part with the keys to the Mustang. "I'll walk from his place," Randy told Jessie. "I can get my car tomorrow. C'mon, tough guy, let's get going and let these two get some sleep. I need some myself, and you need to sleep off that beer."

"Call me in the morning, sweetheart?" Val said, touching Art's arm as they left. Jessie gritted her teeth. He mumbled agreement and they left. Then Jessie turned to Val.

"You slipped? Val, he was beating up on you!"

Val shook her head wearily. "He was going to, I think, but I tried to dodge, and—I tripped over the chair and knocked it over, honestly. Jessie, that's all that happened, I swear. If you hadn't been here, he would have helped me up and it would have been over." She avoided Jessie's eyes, her fingers nervously fiddling with the dangle on her earring.

"It didn't look as though he was helping you up," Jessie said. "And you *think* he was going to hit you— for God's sake, Val, wake up! You don't need that!"

"I need him." Val's face had taken on a set stubbornness. "And I'm not going to give him up. I'll just have to be more careful not to make him mad."

"Yeah, or you'll wind up like Brenda," Jessie growled.

"You think Art killed—Jessie McAllister, you are out of your *mind*!" Val whirled and stomped into her bedroom, slamming the door behind her.

When Jessie came out of her bedroom in the morning, Val was on the phone with Art. From the coo in her voice, it was obvious they weren't fighting. Jessie got some coffee and sat down with the paper, waiting for the call to end.

"Val," Jessie began, after her roommate had hung up. "About what I said last night . . ."

"That business about calling the police?" Val shook her head. "Randy shouldn't have suggested that—it upset Art. He thought Randy was his friend. But it's over now. The whole thing was my own fault; I should never have picked a fight with him about Misty when he was drunk."

"Misty?"

"The brunette, the one . . ." Val's voice died away. *The one she'd seen with Art.* "I shouldn't have said anything."

"Give me a break," Jessie said. "I can't believe you're saying that. You're just going to let him walk all over you?"

There was a flash of temper in Val's eyes for a moment, and Jessie felt hopeful. Then Val looked away.

"He's not walking all over me," Val said. "And there won't be any more Mistys. Or Lauries."

Jessie snorted. "Yeah, right, I suppose he promised you. He's hung over and he's all sorry about it, isn't he? Lot of good that'll do the next time he gets mad."

"He's not going to," Val said softly. This time there was a note of steel under the quiet voice.

"I hope not, for your sake," Jessie said. She'd spent enough time arguing with brick walls for one day. A glance outside showed that Randy's white Toyota was gone. He must have come by early to pick it up. "Anyway, I'm going to the studio. Later."

As she rode down the walk toward the street, she had to repress a shudder. The pyracantha bushes looked battered, with gaps in the thick branches and red smears of crushed berries all over the sidewalk. That was the only visible reminder of Brenda's slow death under those bushes. Jessie didn't know if the ground was still bloodstained and torn up under the leaves, and she didn't stop to look.

All the way to the shop, Jessie kept fighting mental images of those bushes. There was something teasing at the edge of her memory, something she'd been trying to remember ever since that morning when she'd discovered Brenda under them. Whatever it was, it somehow reminded her of Art. That was why she'd been so sure the two murders were related and involved him. In her mind's eye she saw a photo of that first glimpse of Brenda's body, blown up in her imagination to a crisp eight-by-ten. She pictured the bushes, the berries, drops of blood on the leaves and the sidewalk, the limp arm, then gave up. But some detail was missing. Mr. Sweeny had been right, she should have taken a real picture. If she'd only taken a picture, she'd have something solid to show the police.

The police. A squad car passed, and a new thought hit her. Here she was kicking herself for not taking pictures, when the police photographer had taken dozens. Whatever it was that had reminded her of Art might have been something subtle, some minor detail that probably didn't mean anything to the police. But she could explain it to them. If she could spot it.

She rode past Sweeny's, heading for downtown. She hoped Gutierrez would be willing to let her look at the photos.

When he came down to meet her in the lobby, he looked so negative, Jessie almost turned around and left. *He thinks I'm a jealous nut.* That assumption might be logical from his point of view, but the thought turned Jessie's stomach. Despite the look on his face, his greeting was neutral.

"I had my camera with me when I found Brenda, but I didn't take any pictures," she began once they were seated in the same interview room they'd used before.

"I thought you always took pictures," he said. His tone of voice clearly reserved judgment.

"I—just couldn't," she said.

His expression thawed slightly. "That's not surprising. Does it bother you? It shouldn't. I know you were talking about becoming a professional photographer, but even a cop gets shook up if it's someone he knows. And you aren't a pro yet, and you aren't a cop. It's normal to be upset when you find a body."

"That's not it." Jessie shook her head hard. "There was something there, something on the ground by Brenda, and I can't remember what it was. But it made me think of Art, whatever it was." She hesitated for a moment before concluding, "I thought maybe you could let me see the pictures your photographer took, and then maybe I'd remember." She sat back, waiting for a reaction.

There was none, just another of the detective's deadpan stares. *He must practice them in front of the mirror*, Jessie thought irritably. Normal people would show some reaction. After a moment he spoke.

"There's nothing in the photo you wouldn't have seen at the time," he said. "I don't see any problem with your examining it. We're satisfied Mr. Ducas didn't have anything to do with Ms. Wolinsky's death, but maybe if you remember what made you think of him, it will help us find the killer."

Why didn't they think Art was involved? Jessie wanted to ask the question, but she knew all she'd get in response would be another of Gutierrez's bland looks. She waited while he sent for the file.

When it came, she almost dropped the first picture. It was a close-up of pyracantha branches and berries, and torn and bloody earth, but Brenda's body wasn't visible. "Is this . . ." She broke off the question. She really didn't want to look at close-ups of a corpse, but without the body, the scene was completely different.

"The paramedics moved the body when they attempted resuscitation," he said, seeming to read her mind. "They may have shifted a few other things before we got there. See anything that helps?"

Jessie studied that picture for several minutes, then the rest of them. There were the branches and berries and blood, just as she remembered. But there was something missing beside the body. Finally she dropped the last picture and shook her head. Her shoulders slumped.

"It's not there," she said. "Whatever it was isn't in the pictures. It was little, I know that. Maybe one of the paramedics picked it up?"

"Ummmm," he muttered, his eyes fixed on the picture Jessie had dropped. "They wouldn't have picked anything up, but—little, you said." He stared at the photo, and she remembered what he'd said before about the paramedics. *Just two or three more people to walk all over the evidence.*

"Did you ever almost remember something?" Jessie grimaced. "It's like an itch I can't reach."

"Well, if you think of what it was, be sure to call me." Gutierrez stacked the photos neatly and put them back in the manila envelope.

She hesitated for a moment. The detective seemed to believe her this time. Maybe he'd answer a question after all.

"Like I said, it reminded me of Art," she said. "Why don't you think he's involved?"

"We checked his schedule," Gutierrez said. "He had an early class, and the attendance book says he was there."

But that doesn't mean anything, Jessie thought. She knew Art's schedule, and the 7 A.M. lecture was one of the classes he cut whenever he wanted to. The graduate assistant who taught the class always marked Art present, whether he was or not. Art had joked about sleeping through it more than once.

"He could have cut class," Jessie began.

"He's not under suspicion," the detective cut her off. He paused, then continued in a less abrupt tone. "Maybe he's been rotten to your roommate."

Like knocking her around, Jessie thought.

"But that's no excuse for trying to get him in trouble on a murder case," Gutierrez went on. "All that does is hamper the investigation. If you have any real evidence for us, I'll be happy to hear it. I think you did see something, some little thing. Maybe it did remind you of Ducas. Like I said, if you remember what it was, call me. But you've told us about your suspicions now, and we don't need to hear them again."

There wasn't much else to say. He escorted her down to the lobby, repeated that she should call if she remembered what she'd seen, and stood there watching as she walked out the door.

*   *   *

By the time she got back to Sweeny's, she was half an hour late.

"I'm sorry, I wanted to see the pictures the police took."

"You've thought of something?" He shook his head as she explained how different the scene had looked with Brenda gone.

"Next time, take the picture," he said. Then he hurried to add, "I don't mean the next time you find a dead body. Let's hope you never have that dubious pleasure again. I mean the next time you find anything unusual, anything you might want to remember. You're sure there was something missing?"

"I'm sure," Jessie said gloomily. "But I still can't remember what it was, so the whole trip was a waste of time. And it made me late for work."

"No harm done," he said. He went into the darkroom, leaving her to handle the gallery and any customers who wandered in. Sweeny's was mainly an art-photography studio and gallery, and sometimes people came in wanting to purchase one of Jack's distinctive southwestern studies. Several of his photos were hung at the Center for Creative Photography on campus, and Jessie always felt a thrill when she saw them. She was working in one of the best studios in the country.

It was a slow morning, and she decided to develop the pictures she'd taken of Art and Misty. Jessie didn't intend ever to repeat the error she'd made when she'd

101

found Brenda. From now on she'd take pictures no matter what. And developing the film was part of the job. *Besides, maybe Misty will get him mad next*, she thought. It was a morbid idea, but if Misty pushed too hard, the way Laurie had, she'd be next on the list. It was amazing Art hadn't gotten tired of Val, with her assumptions about a golden future together. Maybe he was using her to ward off others, like some girls wore a phony engagement ring to keep creeps at a distance.

She finished making prints, leaving them in the dryer while she made an appointment for one long-standing client. After that some tourists came in and wanted Jessie to tell them the history of each of the prints in the gallery. They took their time, finally purchasing one small print of two Tohono O'odham women harvesting saguaro fruit. Someone else came in looking for film. That happened several times a day. Sweeny's didn't sell cameras or equipment or do much developing except custom work and Jack's own photographs. Jessie referred the would-be customer to a drugstore. By the time she was able to study the pictures of Art and Misty, it was after twelve and Jack had left for lunch.

There wasn't anything unusual in the photos, but she hadn't expected to find anything. The only important thing about them was that they showed Art with yet another girl. Jessie got one of the envelopes they used for prints and labeled it "ART" in block capitals. She slid the photos in and fastened it, wondering as she did if there would ever be any need to take it to Gutierrez. She hoped not.

A shadow fell across her desk as she started to put the envelope away, and Art's voice said, "What's that, your private photo collection of me? Let me see." Jessie looked up. Art stood over her, an unpleasant sneer on his face as he reached for the envelope.

8

"In your dreams," Jessie snapped, moving the envelope out of Art's reach. She thought fast. "These are from the new exhibit at the student union."

"You sure?" Art said, his sneer more open. "I saw you following me all over campus. You couldn't take your eyes off me. And it's got my name on the envelope."

"*Works* of 'art.' Which you aren't, no matter what you think." She opened the drawer and put the envelope inside in one swift movement. "Just because you *think* you see your name on something doesn't give you the right to go snooping through someone's private property." There was a click as she shut the drawer all the way. Oh, great, the damned thing had locked again. She usually left the drawer open a little, since it was hard to unlock. She'd have to get the key later from Mr. Sweeny. Although it might be just as well to leave it locked for a while.

"Don't give me that," he said. Jessie flinched, then hoped he hadn't noticed. "If it was just that junk they've got hanging in the coffee shop, you wouldn't be hiding the pictures." He came around the end of the desk and tried to pull the drawer open, but it didn't budge.

"It's locked," she said, managing to keep her voice calm.

"I can tell that," he snarled. He glared down at her. "Unlock it. I want to see those pictures."

"I don't have the key," Jessie said. "You can wait for Mr. Sweeny if you want to. He has the key, but I don't have to show you anything. Any pictures I take are my business, not yours."

"When they're pictures of me—"

"Even then. Not that they are," she added hastily. "Just like you to assume you're the center of the universe."

"Why were you following me around?" Art demanded. "You never did explain that."

"I was just watching to see how you'd hurt Val next," Jessie said. "I found out last night, didn't I?"

Art suddenly lost his sneer and seemed almost to shrink. "Yeah, well," he mumbled, "that's really what I came about. I acted pretty stupid last night, and I'm sorry."

"Try apologizing to Val."

"I did," he said. For just an instant there was a flash in his eyes of the temper he'd been showing moments before, and Jessie felt her stomach knot in fear for her roommate. Had Val had another fight with Art? Then the expression faded, and Art continued. "We're cool, but she said I ought to apologize to you and Randy as well. Blame the beer."

"Maybe you should leave it alone, if it's going to affect you that way," Jessie said.

"Yeah, well . . ." He left the sentence hanging.

"It didn't sound like you were very sorry when you came in here," she said. "Trying to bully me like that."

"Look, I'm sorry, all right? Keep the damned—I mean, they're your pictures, keep 'em. You don't have to sic Randy on me this time." He smiled at her, an artificial grin that she felt like slapping off his face. "I'll be good."

"Just be gone," Jessie said. Art's trying to be funny about his drunken rage was worse in a way than the anger itself.

"Yeah. Catch you later." He walked out of the store as Jessie thought, *Not if I see you coming, you won't.*

A few minutes later Jack Sweeny got back, and Jessie felt her neck muscles relax. She must have been more uptight during the confrontation with Art than she'd realized. Nothing had happened beyond his lame apology, but she wasn't going to leave those pictures in the drawer. The photos of Art and Brenda never had shown up, and Jessie didn't have much faith in the flimsy lock if Art decided he really wanted to see them. *Good thing his name isn't Bob or something*, she thought wryly. She asked Jack to open the drawer; it wasn't the first time she'd closed it all the way by accident.

She retrieved the envelope, then rummaged through the clutter. She really had taken pictures of the exhibit at the student-union building, but the photos weren't anything special. She'd just tossed the pictures into the junk drawer. "Junk" was the right word, she decided as she finally found them under a tangle of rubber bands and paper clips. It was almost as bad as her work-file box back at the apartment. She really should sort through all this garbage, but not now. She had classes, and she was going to be lucky to get to the first one on time. She took the photos of Art and Misty from the envelope and put the ones from the student art show in their place. Then she left the envelope on the desk. No sense making Art break the drawer open if he decided to come back. She hesitated for a moment, then put the original pictures in an unmarked envelope and placed it back in the drawer. This time when she closed it all the way, it wasn't by accident.

As soon as she got back to the apartment, Val demanded, "Did Art come by and apologize?"

"Yeah," Jessie said. "He said you told him to."

"He didn't have to tell you that." For a moment

Val's lips tightened, then she shrugged and relaxed. "Oh, well, as long as he did it. We can just forget the whole thing now—it's over."

"Over? Val, what makes you think it won't happen again, or something else just as bad?"

"We had a long talk this morning," Val answered. She looked the same as always, pretty and soft, her intelligence camouflaged by her looks, which were right off the cover of a cheap romance. But for once, her voice had lost its breathless sound, and the determination could be heard. Jessie had seen Val's temper in action a few times, but she'd never heard that tone before.

"Are you two breaking up?" Jessie asked, after it became obvious Val wasn't going to continue.

"Of course not. We just had to come to an understanding, and we did." Val flashed about two hundred watts' worth of smile. "Valentine's Day is in ten days, and I suspect we'll have a little announcement to make then." The smug expression on her face as she glanced down at her ringless left hand made it obvious what the announcement would be.

I don't believe it, Jessie thought. Art's behavior hardly indicated he was ready for marriage, and Randy had told her Art's long-range plans didn't include Val, no matter what she thought. Jessie thought about the photos of Misty, but she knew better than to mention them. Instead she said, "And the other night never happened, is that it? Val, that's stupid. You're going to get hurt again if you keep acting this way."

"Is that supposed to be a warning or something?" Val asked. "More of that crap about Art being a killer? Talk about stupid. That's about as ridiculous as anything I ever heard. Why would he kill a couple of girls he barely knew?"

"He knew Laurie a lot better than he ever admitted to you," Jessie said bluntly. "She was pushing him, demanding too much. She wanted him to dump you for her—"

Val snorted. "That doesn't surprise me. But you'll notice he's still here."

"—and she pushed a little too hard and he got angry," Jessie went on. She ignored the interruption. "Brenda started hassling him about her, and I have a hunch she knew more than she told me."

"What do you mean?" That had caught Val's attention.

"For God's sake, Val, who do you *think* told me Art was ready to drop you? Brenda knew all about it. She told me she tried to warn Laurie about Art's temper, but Laurie wouldn't listen. And you haven't listened either." Jessie took a deep breath. "His temper *should* scare you, even if it doesn't. I've told the police what Brenda said about Art taking steroids. If someone else turns up dead, I think they'll look a little harder at him." The expression in Val's eyes should have dropped Jessie in her tracks. For a moment Jessie hesitated about the rest of it, the missing photos, his knowledge of Brenda's jogging route, all the little bits of evidence that, piece by piece, added up in her mind to a verdict of *guilty* against Art Ducas. Then she went on. By the time she had finished, Val looked shaken. *Good*, Jessie thought. *Maybe that got through to her.*

"I'm sorry if this hurts," Jessie concluded, "but now do you see why I've been trying to warn you? I may be wrong, but there's too much that hasn't been explained."

"I don't want to believe you," Val said in a low voice. "And I don't. I'm going to talk to Art again, and I'll ask him, but I don't believe it. All right, maybe you're just worried about me, but you're wrong."

"Even if I am, that still doesn't make Art a prize catch, and you'd better not count on a wedding."

"Art's mine. And we're getting married!" With that, Val stood up and left, slamming the front door behind her.

The next few days passed quietly. Val didn't make any more references to getting a ring on Valentine's Day, but she went back to spending a lot of time with Art, acting the same gooey way she had before. The first time he showed up at the apartment, Jessie regarded him warily, but if Val had actually told him about her suspicions, he gave no indication of it. He made his usual jokes, ate pizza, and complained about forgetting his things again. That time he managed to take some of his junk home, but he left an elastic knee brace he'd been carrying. Val called him about it later, teasing him. Things were back to normal.

The lack of change frustrated Jessie. She didn't want to see the two dead girls forgotten, their killer walking around free. The envelope labeled "ART" and filled with innocuous pictures of paintings was still on Jessie's desk at Sweeny's. No one had bothered it, and Art hadn't been back to the shop. She was stymied.

The first inkling Jessie had that things weren't as peaceful as they seemed came when she finally decided to organize her work-file box. She pulled it out from under the table and dumped it. Odd. There wasn't as much in it as she'd thought. She started to list the contents in a notebook. As she worked, her confusion grew. The pile of stuff worth keeping was much too small. Most of what was in the box was just junk. She listed some pictures from an early trip to the Desert Museum, then looked for the ones she'd taken the day she'd gone with Jack. The day after Laurie's murder, she thought somberly. She'd gotten a good picture of the jaguar, but it wasn't here.

"Jessie, have you seen my other earring?" Val came out of her bedroom fastening an earring in her right ear. "I can't find it anyplace."

Jessie shook her head. She recognized the earring. It was one Art had given Val for Christmas—long red bead dangles that were striking against Val's blond hair.

"Haven't seen it," Jessie told her roommate. Val made a face and unhooked the thin gold wire again. The dangles were always falling off. "I seem to be missing some stuff myself. Have you taken any of my photos?" It was a foolish question—Val had never shown any interest in Jessie's work. But now that she'd tallied them, there were quite a few prints missing, and at least one folder of negatives.

"Why on earth would I do that?" Val pulled the single earring off and looked at it in disgust. "Damn, these would have gone great with my outfit. Maybe the lapis—I haven't touched your box, but Art kicked it accidentally the other night, and it went all over. I thought we got them all up, but maybe not. You might look under the couch. I told you it was a bad idea to store that under the table." She shrugged and went back into her own room to get the other earrings.

Jessie stared after her for a moment. Art. Art had kicked the box "accidentally." And now there were photos missing. She got the flashlight and poked under the couch for a moment, but as she expected, there was nothing under it but dust balls. Art had no reason to want photographs of the Desert Museum's birds, but she doubted if he was after those, anyway. He had probably just grabbed as many pictures as possible while pretending to pick them up. He knew she'd taken photos when she tailed him around campus, and he'd already stolen the ones of Brenda. He must be after any pictures she'd taken of him.

Over the next few days, the phone rang several times, always when she was alone in the apartment, and the caller would hang up immediately. She felt as though someone was watching her, but she could never spot Art doing so, or anyone else for that matter. One morning her bike wasn't where she'd left it, and by the time she found it, she was late for her English class.

The phone calls were nothing serious—no threats, just the type of thing that could be dismissed as a prank. The misplaced bike could even be absentmindedness on her part. She could imagine the reception she'd get from Gutierrez if she was foolish enough to tell him. But Jessie was positive that Art was responsible, and she thought she knew why. It was a warning, a much more subtle warning than his earlier crude threats. The fact that the harassment was so indirect bothered her more than anything else. By now Art knew that she wouldn't be bullied, and that she wouldn't hesitate about calling the police. He was carefully avoiding obvious menace, but still letting her know that she could be next on his list.

The question was, What about Val? She still cooed at Art over the phone, calling him "sweetheart" until Jessie felt like gagging. And she was constantly making confident assumptions about the wonderful future she and Art would share when he started playing pro ball. But sometimes Jessie saw a different Val, one she'd never seen before. She looked pensive and was quieter than normal, and Jessie caught her once when she looked as if she'd been crying. She wasn't sure, but she thought she'd heard Val crying at night as well. Val might be seeing the truth at last.

Jessie thought she'd caught Art in a foolish mistake at one point. There was a slip of folded paper inside her English textbook, and she opened it while the instructor was lecturing. There were only a few words on it: *Minding other people's business is a dangerous hobby.* She looked at it, trying to see if there was anything unusual about it. It was from a computer printer. Typewriters were as unique as snowflakes, no two alike, but the printers used with computers couldn't be "fingerprinted" the way typewriters could. The thought of fingerprints made her drop the page, but then she picked it up again. Art wasn't stupid. He certainly would know enough to avoid leaving fingerprints. It was a single anonymous line that could have come from anyplace. Even so, it was the first concrete threat Jessie had seen, and she carefully refolded the paper and stuck it back in her English notebook. Even if it wasn't worth taking to Gutierrez, it was worth saving.

The note may have been worth saving, but she didn't manage to hold on to it for long. Jessie headed for the library after English, planning on doing some studying. She left her books on a table and went to get more from the stacks. When she returned to the table, Art and Val were standing there.

"There was a call from your boss," Val told her. "I

thought I should pass it along right away. He wants you to work tonight—he's got some sort of banquet, and he promised to let some people look at his work at the studio."

Such emergencies had happened before. Occasionally, for longtime clients, Jack would open the gallery at night, but this time it looked as though he couldn't be there himself. Jessie felt pleased that he trusted her to handle this situation on her own.

"How'd you find me?" she asked her roommate.

"You've been studying more in the library for the last month than you have at the apartment," Val said. "We just split up and hunted for you."

After they left, Jessie wasn't at all surprised to find the paper missing. There was no point in searching for it. Art could have dropped it into any of the numerous recycling boxes scattered throughout the library. No one would have noticed, and there were too many for Jessie to dig through. If she tried it, she'd be there half the night.

Rather than go home for dinner before work, Jessie stopped at the Snack Shack for a sandwich and took it with her. When she reached the studio, she let herself in, then turned on the lights in the gallery and sat down with her sandwich and soda. The generous sandwich was the same as usual, but it tasted dry. She'd thought, for once, she had something concrete, something to prove that all the little things that had been happening weren't her imagination. Now that proof

116

was gone. Art hadn't said a word while they were in the library, but he must have felt like laughing his head off at her. He'd done it again, and each time his message got clearer. *Minding other people's business is a dangerous hobby.*

But it wasn't *other* people's—it was hers. Val was her roommate, Laurie had been her classmate. She'd been the one to find Brenda. As always, the vague memory stirred as she thought of that, the missing piece of the puzzle, but this time it was just a momentary twinge. The murders were her business as much as anyone else's. She'd been involved since the first night, when she'd recognized Laurie. The threats just made it all more personal.

The customers were twenty minutes late. When they arrived, they took their time in the gallery, studying each photo carefully. When the phone rang, Jessie grabbed it quickly before the answering machine could catch it, figuring Mr. Sweeny would be calling to check on the customers. Instead there was silence, followed by a soft click.

For a moment Jessie felt frightened; then anger replaced the fear. For the anonymous caller to be calling at night, at work, was a new trick. But of course Art knew she'd be here. He was with Val when she gave Jessie the message, and he'd probably been with her when she'd taken the phone call from Jack. This was just another bit of harassment, a new way to scare her and warn her off. And she wasn't going to let him succeed.

The couple finally left around eleven, leaving a check for Jack to hold a couple of prints they wanted. After they were gone, Jessie shut off the lights in the gallery and back room. She looked at her book bag, debating—but she was too tired. The day had been long enough already—she'd never do any homework tonight. Jessie shoved the bag under the counter; she could pick it up on her way to campus in the morning. She grabbed her camera case and got ready to leave when the telephone rang explosively beside her.

She jumped, her heart doing double time, but then decided to let it ring. If the caller was Jack, she could explain in the morning—but she wasn't picking up the phone. It rang three times; then there was a loud click as Jack's recorded voice asked the caller to leave a message. A short, high-pitched beep was followed by a brief silence, ending in a click and a dial tone.

Jessie gritted her teeth. She was *not* going to let Art spook her by doing this! She made sure the front door was locked, then unchained her bike and started for home. A few dogs barked late-night greetings as she passed, and the yellow cat that collected handouts from the local restaurants and cafés crossed her path, tail held high. The temperature had dropped into the thirties, but despite the chill, the clear, quiet night relaxed her.

The intersection at University Boulevard was empty, with no traffic in either direction. Ignoring the red light, Jessie swung diagonally across the intersection, not even slowing down as she went around the corner. When she reached the far side, the sudden roar of an engine behind her almost made her lose her balance.

She looked over her shoulder. A car, with only its yellow parking lights visible, was speeding around the corner, and heading right for her.

9

Jessie whipped her head back around in terror. Adrenaline gave her an extra spurt of energy as she pedaled for the sidewalk. The car, a heavy sedan, fishtailed as it came around the corner, swinging wide onto Jessie's side of the street. She reached the curb and threw herself sideways off the bike just as the car got there. The bike dropped beside the curb as she rolled behind one of the trees that lined the street. There was a metallic screech as the car clipped the back fender of the fallen bike, fishtailed again, then roared up University Boulevard.

This time Jessie's instincts were working. She was unzipping her camera case even before she stopped rolling. She flicked the lens cap off with one finger and frantically adjusted the focus, managing to get just one shot before the car squealed around the corner at Sixth Avenue, its tires burning.

For a moment longer Jessie just lay there in the dirt, too shaken to move. Then she sat up, groaning as she did so. Now that everything was over, she could feel the scrapes from her rough landing, and her left shin throbbed where she'd hit it on the frame of her bike as she dived off. She'd wrenched her shoulder as well. The whole thing had taken no more than a few seconds.

She checked her camera, worried more about it than about her own injuries. Fortunately the lens was intact, and the camera and flash unit both seemed to be working. The heavy padded case had given her equipment more cushioning than the dirt had given her. She felt around on the ground for the lens cap, but she couldn't find it—a minor loss. Jessie zipped the camera back into its case with a feeling of relief. This time, she'd gotten a picture.

Her bike was another story. When Jessie picked it up from the gutter, there was a creak of protesting metal. No way could she ride it—the back wheel was bent, and the fender was pushed up against the tire. She'd have to push it home. She hooked her camera case over her neck and started walking, but the rear wheel of the bike just skidded along the pavement, unable to turn. Jessie grabbed the seat and lifted the back wheel off the ground. Pushing the bike like an ungainly wheelbarrow, she started once more for home.

At least she had only a few blocks to go. The trip would have taken just a few minutes if she'd been riding. Half pushing and half carrying the bike, with frequent stops to readjust her awkward load, she made the distance in close to twenty. When she finally reached the apartment, her muscles were trembling from fatigue. The trip would have been easier had the front tire, rather than the rear, been messed up. As it was, she'd nearly dropped the bike several times as the front wheel turned behind her. Her shins were covered with bruises, and she thought she'd lost some skin from banging into the pedals. She didn't bother to chain the bike this time; instead she propped it up against the wall and left it.

As soon as she closed and locked the door behind her, she let out a sigh of relief. Val was in the living room lying on the couch in her fuzzy pink bathrobe, watching a video. She glanced up as Jessie came in and did a double take at the condition of Jessie's clothes. "What on earth happened to you?" She hit the pause button.

"I fell off my bike," Jessie said shortly. She wasn't going to tell Val the whole story without more evidence. Evidence that she might have right there in her camera.

"You're too good a rider to just 'fall off,'" Val protested. "What happened?"

"I told you, I fell. A car got a little too close when I turned the corner off Fourth." Jessie looked down at herself. The dirt and the rips in her jeans looked pretty bad. She knew there were bloody patches on her shins, as well. The danger would have been much worse if the driver of that car had succeeded in hitting her.

The driver. It had to be Art. "I thought you were going out tonight with Art," Jessie said. "Early night, or did you have a fight?" Mentally she added, *Or did he just not want any witnesses?*

"Something came up, he couldn't make it," Val said. "Look, why don't I fix you a cup of tea or something? Pushing that bike must have been grim."

"Just call it aerobic exercise." Jessie forced a grin. "But I wouldn't recommend it as a real fun thing to do."

A while later, Jessie was soaking in a hot bubble bath, drinking a mug of herbal tea. Some of the knots in her back had unkinked. Her shins were as bad as she'd expected, with bruises already visible by the time she got her pants off. She ran more hot water, letting the excess trickle down the overflow while she thought. At first she'd wondered if it really *had* been an accident, since Val had said earlier she was going out with Art. Besides, it hadn't been his familiar red Mustang. But he'd canceled the date, and he'd done so *after* he found out Jessie would be working late. Laurie's murderer had driven a stolen car, and Jessie was willing to bet this one would be stolen as well. Art would never risk damage to his precious convertible, or risk it being seen.

If the car was stolen, the photograph she'd managed to take might not be worth much. But at least she had one this time.

The next day, as soon as her final class was over, she headed to Sweeny's on foot. An examination of the bike had confirmed her initial damage estimate. She'd have to have Randy drop it off at the shop, and she'd be lucky if it didn't cost a couple hundred dollars to fix. By the time she reached the studio, her legs were screaming. Despite the long hot soak the night before, they were still sore. She'd almost chosen a skirt that morning rather than her usual jeans. She didn't look forward to heavy fabric rubbing against all the raw places. But she'd put the skirt back; it was too chilly for bare legs, and she didn't want to spend the day explaining what had happened.

"What's wrong with you?" Jack said as she came in.

Jessie limped over to her desk and collapsed in the chair thankfully. "I banged my bike up last night, and my legs got a little crumpled as well," she said. She eased the fabric up on her left leg, thinking the bleeding had started again—but it only felt that way. "I'll be all right, it's just skin."

"Hey, where would you be without skin?" Jack asked with a grin, then answered his own question. "All over the sidewalk."

Jessie groaned theatrically, knowing that was the response Jack expected to his bad jokes, but this time she really didn't find it funny. All over the sidewalk and street was just about where she would have been, if Art had hit her. Just like Laurie.

"Good job with the Chazwitzes last night," Jack said, changing the subject. "They're taking two of the prints. How late did they stay?"

"Till around eleven," Jessie answered. He winced.

"Sorry. If I'd known they were going to take that long, I could have gotten over here myself. Hate to make you work that much overtime on a class night."

"It's all right," she assured him. Jack's presence probably wouldn't have stopped Art. The real question was, Had he been trying to kill her, or was it just another, more sinister, threat?

As soon as she could, Jessie developed the film. The single picture was blurry and at an angle, but enlarging it revealed the numbers on the license plate. She grinned in triumph; Jack would be proud of her. The car was a Buick; she could make out enough of the insignia to tell that. It was a dark shape, the parking lights making a blur of light on the exposure, but the small light on the license-plate frame showed the number JOC 101. The number was eerily appropriate—a jock had been driving.

The next question was what to do with it? She debated with herself for a while. Finally she took the enlargement over to Jack and told him the whole story.

"And you didn't report it?" he demanded, horrified. "You should have come back to the studio and called the cops."

"All I wanted to do was get home," Jessie said. He was right, she should have reported it, but she'd been too shaken to think of that. "I guess I shouldn't have moved the bike either."

A snort of disgust was his only response, but he shut the shop long enough to drive her down to headquarters. "Call me when you get done," he told her. Then he headed back to the studio.

She hadn't intended to speak to Gutierrez, but when she reached the window to be admitted to the building, the same policewoman was on duty, and she recognized Jessie. Within a few minutes the detective had joined her down in the lobby.

"What's on your mind this time, Jessie?" His voice held a note of resigned patience that infuriated her. Damn it, did he think she was a total idiot? But one look at his expression answered that: he did.

"Someone tried to run me down late last night," she began.

His face grew more alert. "Last night? Did you get a good look at the car?" He led the way to the elevators as he spoke. "What time did this happen, and why didn't you report it?"

"It was around eleven," she said, following him out of the elevator and down the hall. This time he led her to a different interview room, one slightly larger than the one she'd been in before. "I'm sure it was Art, but it wasn't his car."

"Describe the car," he instructed, taking out a notepad. He ignored Jessie's comment about Art.

"I can do better than that." She reached inside her windbreaker and got out the photo. Handing it to him, she said, "I had my camera with me. The car didn't have its lights on, just its parks, but you can make out the number, and the emblem looks like it says Buick."

"Eighty-nine Buick Regal," he said absently, his eyes still fastened on the picture. "I'll get someone started on this." He stepped out, the photo still in his hand. When he returned a few minutes later, there was a disgusted look on his face.

"Dead end," he announced. "The car was reported stolen this morning, and they just turned it up near campus. They've already checked for prints—nada." He sat back down. "Since the owner's a sweet little old granny who reminds me of my mother, and who probably goes to bed before nine P.M., I doubt if she's the one who was driving, and she has no idea when it was stolen. She just found it missing when she wanted to go shopping this morning and reported it."

"Of course it was stolen," Jessie said. "I knew that. The car that hit Laurie was, too. That convertible of Art's is too noticeable, he'd never use it."

"All right, suppose you start from the beginning," Gutierrez said.

"I was at the studio. Mr. Sweeny had some special customers coming in, and he couldn't be there." She went through the entire story, including the phone calls. She even pulled up the leg of her pants to show him the bruises and scrapes. They looked ugly, purple and puffy, and the worst of the scraped patches was scarlet.

Whatever he was thinking, Gutierrez said only, "I wish you'd called us last night, Jessie." His voice was surprisingly gentle for once. "It sounds like you were pretty shook up."

"Shook up, and hurting, and scared out of my mind," she admitted. "All I wanted to do was get home. And the bike's a mess."

"We might be able to match scratches or paint with Mrs. Montoya's car and your bike, but there's no point in it," he said. "The photo tells us that was the car, and you're not hurt"—he broke off as she started to protest and rephrased the statement—"not *seriously* hurt. No fingerprints, and Mrs. Montoya left the key in the ignition so she could find it. Traffic's already spoken to her about that. Evidently she's been doing it for years. She said nothing ever happened before."

Gutierrez sighed and stared at the picture again. "There's nothing to indicate who was driving the car, unfortunately. I'm hoping something will show."

"Art broke a date with my roommate last night," Jessie said.

"That's not a crime," Gutierrez said, shaking his

129

head. "Jessie, will you drop this vendetta of yours against Ducas? You've almost convinced me that both deaths may be related. *May* be, I said. But I'm convinced that there's something you haven't told me that's the key to the whole case, and you're so busy with your little feud with your roommate's boyfriend, you—"

"It's not a vendetta," Jessie interrupted him. "I've told you everything I know, everything that's happened that I have any proof for. You're not interested in what I think, that's obvious." She stood up. "I may as well go back to work. This isn't doing any good. Can I call Mr. Sweeny for a ride?"

"Maybe I can find you a lift," he said, standing also. On the way down in the elevator, he asked her one last question. "Have you remembered what was missing in the photographs of the murder scene?"

"No," she said. The memory still teased, like the name of a song she couldn't recall.

When they got down to the lobby, Gutierrez found a squad car just going on duty and arranged to have her dropped off at the studio. As she left, he said, "Take care, Jessie." His tired face was troubled. "No more going out late at night by yourself, and please, open your eyes. I'm afraid you're going to just keep watching Ducas while someone else sneaks up behind you."

"Don't worry," she said grimly. "I still think it's him, but I'll be careful."

"With everyone, not just with him," Gutierrez said.

"All right. With everyone." The uniformed officer held the door open for her, and she followed him out to the squad car.

The squad car dropped her off at the studio. Jessie described the interview to Mr. Sweeny before she got back to work. If he noticed her dissatisfaction with Gutierrez's reaction, he said nothing. After an hour or so, he took her home, telling her to get some rest.

The apartment was empty. There was a note on the refrigerator door from Val asking Jessie to tell Art she'd be home by six thirty. Restless, Jessie prowled around the apartment, limping occasionally as her shin throbbed. Despite Jack's advice to relax, she was still too uptight, both from the previous night and from the talk with Gutierrez. In one way the detective was right—she didn't have a scrap of real evidence. Not the sort that would stand up in court, the kind that could be put under a microscope or measured and weighed. She'd tried to get some evidence before by tailing Art, but that had been a farce. All she'd managed to accomplish was to look foolish and to redirect Art's temper toward her. If last night was the result of that, Jessie didn't want a repeat performance.

She stopped by the window, looking out from behind the curtain without really seeing anything. There had to be *something* she could do. She was tired of being a target. Her eyes fastened on the crumpled bicycle propped up against the wall. She could have been killed. She shook her head and let the curtain drop back into place. No sense brooding about it. She'd better do something about the bike, though. She went over and called Randy.

"Wish you'd said something earlier in the day," he said after Jessie had explained the problem with the bike. She glossed over how it had been damaged. "I'm supposed to meet Art in twenty minutes in the weight room. I could pick it up in the morning, if that'd help any."

"Just as long as I don't have to lug the thing myself," Jessie said. "There's a bike shop down on Speedway. If I just leave it, can you drop it off there sometime tomorrow?"

"No problem, Jessie. Love you." He hung up, and she resumed her prowl around the apartment.

Even Randy didn't believe her, she thought despondently. He'd seen the pictures of Art's face twisted in rage, he'd even stopped Art the night he'd gotten drunk and shoved Val down; but he was going to work out with Art as though nothing had happened. As though Laurie and Brenda had never existed.

They were going to lift weights. For some reason, that fact stuck in her mind. Now, why was that important? Jessie flopped down on the couch, staring at the blank TV screen while she thought about it. A pile of Art's junk lay on top of the set, waiting for him to remember it. Slowly a plan began to take shape in

Jessie's mind like a print forming on contact paper. At first there was just a blur; then the plan took shape all at once. She could see it clearly in her mind.

Jessie had read a lot of mystery novels, and she loved watching old detective shows on TV. Tailing a suspect wasn't the only thing detectives did. Art had a habit of leaving his belongings scattered around, even in his own apartment. He might have something there that would be proof. Maybe a letter from Brenda threatening him. Or maybe his supply of steroids.

Weights. *That* was why she kept thinking of Art and Randy in the weight room! They'd be tied up for at least a couple of hours. Jessie had gone with Val to drop off things at Art's apartment a few times, and she knew where Art hid his spare key. If she left right now, she'd have plenty of time to poke around before Art got home.

She rummaged in her work file for a moment. It was still as messy as ever. When she'd realized there were things missing, she'd gotten distracted and had never finished sorting through it. But she thought she remembered . . . She let out a yip of triumph as she pulled out a pair of thin plastic gloves. She sometimes used them to keep from ruining her manicure when she was developing pictures. They were thin enough to work in, and they'd keep her from leaving fingerprints. She stuffed them inside her camera case, made sure she had extra film and her macro lens, and left the apartment.

As she stepped outside, her right leg cramped suddenly. *Oh, great.* She bent down and massaged the calf muscle. At this rate, Art would be back home before she even got there. His apartment on Helen Street was almost twenty blocks away, and her legs still hadn't recovered. She straightened up as a neighbor came down the walk. It was one of the guys from the next unit, the ones who played their radio too loud. He nodded as he went past, and she made a fast decision.

"Pat? Could you do me a favor?"

"I'm Paul," he said, smiling, "but you can still ask."

"Do you have a car? I need to get someplace, and I've got cramps in my legs from falling off my bike yesterday."

A few minutes later they pulled out of the parking lot in Paul's dirty white pickup. Jessie was grateful for the ride. Even if her legs hadn't been hurting, the walk would have cut into her time for—well, for snooping. There was no other word for it.

This was only the second time she'd talked with Paul, and she was reminded once more of how impersonal a big school or city could be, even a city as friendly as Tucson. Big enough that you didn't know your neighbors the way you did in a small town, impersonal enough that you could die and not be missed. But right now anonymity worked in her favor. It was unlikely that any of Art's neighbors would notice or care about her letting herself into his apartment.

Still, she looked around before she got out the plastic gloves and slipped them on. Art didn't live in a complex like her own, but in one of several small buildings—converted tourist cabins that were now used as apartments. She went directly to the fourth rock in a line that marked off a scraggly garden. The key was there, just as she remembered.

She hesitated for a moment before letting herself in. If Art hadn't gone with Randy for some reason and was actually inside, "embarrassed" wouldn't begin to describe how she'd feel.

She slipped the plastic gloves off and pounded on the door with her knuckles, careful not to let a fingertip brush the weathered wood. After a moment she knocked again. There was still no answer. She put the gloves back on and let herself in. What she had done was illegal. It was breaking and entering, but right now she didn't care.

She started in the small living room, but besides the couch, VCR, sound system, and an amazing collection of tapes and CDs, there wasn't much to see. The apartment had surprised her the first time she'd been in it. Outside, it looked like a dump in need of a coat of paint. The "lawn" consisted of a few sick clumps of Bermuda grass and bare dirt. But inside, the place was much nicer than the one she shared with Val. Jessie eyed the comfortable sofa, guessing that Art himself must have furnished the place. She slipped her hand between the soft cushions but found nothing except some loose change and the sort of miscellaneous junk that usually accumulates in such places. She glanced through the videos briefly. She recognized some of the titles, but none of them had anything to do with Laurie or Brenda.

Jessie went on into the bedroom. It was cluttered, the bed unmade and random pieces of clothes scattered across the floor. She got her camera out, leaving the case slung around her neck so she wouldn't forget anything when she left, and took several shots of the mess as an overview, then carefully started to search through Art's things. There was nothing unusual in the closet, except Val's green-and-gray sweater that had been missing for weeks. Things usually gravitated to her and Val's apartment, not Art's. Jessie crossed to the dresser and pulled open the top drawer. It was a tangle of jockey shorts and unmatched socks, with odds and ends of junk. One good thing: there was no way Art would notice anything out of place here. Still, she tried to put stuff back in the same general order as she found it. The bottom drawer was empty, as though Art hadn't wanted to bother with bending over that far.

Jessie pushed the drawer back in, leaving it slightly crooked, the way it was before she opened it. Straightening up, she spotted a familiar shape on the floor, wedged between the dresser and the corner. It was Art's Wildcat mascot, identical to the one that had been in Laurie's backpack. Jessie took a picture of it, careful not to touch it or to shift its position. There was no way of knowing if Laurie's had been the original or one of the copies, but it didn't matter. The mascot had focused Jessie's attention on Art and served as the first step in the trail. Art had said he kept the stuffed animal for luck, she recalled. But he didn't seem to care very much about it. She left the toy where it was and turned to the rest of the room.

As the minutes passed, she glanced at her watch more and more frequently. She didn't dare stay too long. Finally, she hit pay dirt. Halfway down a heap of books, she found a cheap photo album. She opened it and bit her tongue to keep from yelling. The first picture in the album was a photo of Laurie in a bikini, signed, *For Art—with all my heart, and the rest of me as well!* Jessie checked her light meter, then adjusted the focus. She made several shots at different exposures, then turned the page.

The album wasn't full, but there were several more pictures of Laurie and Art, individually and together. Some of them were obviously posed shots taken by Laurie herself, including one of Art standing in front of the apartment, wearing nothing but a pair of jeans and a grin. Another one must have been taken by someone else. It showed the interior of a strange apartment, with Art and Laurie locked in a kiss. Jessie got pictures of them all.

She flipped through the rest of the album, but there were only blank pages for the last three quarters of it. Laying her camera down for a moment, she slid the album back into the stack of books after checking that there was nothing else of interest among them. Only a library book caught her attention, with a due date last September. Jessie picked up her camera and stood up.

The pictures proved that Art had been lying about Laurie. She had already known that, but now she could prove to Gutierrez that their relationship hadn't been a casual one- or two-date affair. That might be enough to convince the cops to take another look, but she'd like to find something else as well. She glanced around the bedroom, considering where she should try next, when she heard a car stop outside. She froze, hoping it was a neighbor, but a few moments later she heard a pair of familiar voices outside the door.

Art had come home, and Randy was with him.

Jessie could hear the rattle of the key in the lock, and some muttered curse from Art. In one step she was across the tiny hall and through the bathroom door. She eased it shut behind her just as she heard the front door open. As quietly as she could, she fastened the hook that locked the bathroom door on the inside. The lock looked horribly flimsy, but it might buy her a few precious seconds of time.

She froze as Randy's voice came through the thin panel. "You got anything to put on that knee?" She held her breath as the doorknob moved slightly. Randy's hand must be on it.

"Hell, no." Art's voice was farther away; he was probably on the couch. "Just get me a beer from the fridge. I'll soak the knee later—right now I just want to relax. Damn, that hurts."

The doorknob shifted again as Randy released it. Jessie could hear him going to the kitchen and opening the refrigerator. "I still say you should have said something to Al."

"Yeah, and have the whole circus start up," Art said. He sucked in his breath sharply, as though he'd moved too fast. Jessie could hear each sound clearly. "I just wrenched the damned thing a little."

"Isn't that the knee that was giving you trouble during the season?" Randy asked. There was the sound of a refrigerator closing, and more footsteps.

"I said I'm all *right*," Art snarled. Jessie heard the soft *pop* as the can was opened. The door was so thin, it barely muffled sounds in the apartment. It would splinter if any force was applied at all. She couldn't stay here long without being discovered, and the apartment was too small for her to sneak out while their backs were turned. Besides, Art was in the living room, next to the only door to the outside.

Her camera was still in her hand. She put it back into the case, gritting her teeth at the soft rasp of the zipper. The voices continued from the other room; they must not have heard the tiny sound. She looked around, then stepped lightly across the old-fashioned bathroom to the toilet. Above it, high on the wall, was an uncurtained window. The window wasn't very big, but Jessie was sure she could squeeze through. She'd have to try, anyway. It was the only alternative to staying there and being found. Sooner or later one of them would need the john.

She lowered the lid to the toilet as quietly as she could, then stepped up on it. She could reach the window easily from there, but climbing through would be another thing. She'd have to stand on the back of the tank, and there was a big crack along one side of it slowly dripping water into a coffee can on the floor. The tank might not bear her weight. But she had no choice.

Carefully she opened the latch on the window. The little handle moved easily enough, and without noise. So far, so good. She shifted her camera case so it was slung across her chest, then gently tried to push the window open. It was stuck.

Jessie shoved a little harder. The window still didn't budge, and for the first time she noticed the grunge and buildup of rust on the hinges. This window must not have been opened in years. She shoved again, without results.

It *had* to open, it was the only way out! Desperate, Jessie pushed as hard as she could. The window came open suddenly with a loud shriek of protest. It stuck halfway, but there was enough room for her to squeeze through. Behind her, she heard shouts and the sound of rapid footsteps. She grabbed both sides of the window frame and stepped up on the tank. The door rattled as the hook, stronger than it looked, held for a precious moment. She got one knee on the edge of the window as the tank collapsed under her other foot with a crash of breaking porcelain. Jessie pitched through the window headfirst, barely managing to catch herself on her hands as she fell to the ground. From inside came splintering sounds as the door broke open. She scrambled to her feet and ran across the alley, diving over the low brick wall of someone's backyard, and lay there for a moment trying to control her panting, her legs hurting viciously.

Voices reached her from across the alley. She didn't dare raise her head, but she could tell both of the guys were now at the window. "Dammit, I don't see anyone. Where the hell could he have gotten to so fast?" That was Art, obviously searching for the intruder. Jessie huddled even closer to the ground.

"Never mind that, where's the cutoff valve?" Randy's voice was muffled, and she realized what must have happened. The tank had been knocked off by her weight, and the water must still be flooding out of the broken fixture. She got to her knees and crawled along the wall until she was behind a paloverde tree. Standing, she looked back at Art's apartment. The alley was vacant; they must be dealing with the broken toilet. If it hadn't been for that, they'd be after her by now, and they might get the water shut off at any second. Jessie checked the back of Art's apartment again, then ran as fast as she could toward the next street. No one had seen her; there'd be no way for the guys to know where she'd gone.

She dodged through several alleys and cut through yards, coming out several blocks north of Art's apartment on a quiet residential street. Once she had put some distance between herself and Art's place, she relaxed. Turning left, she headed for home. With luck, she was far enough away that they wouldn't spot her if they came searching. Even so, she kept a wary eye out as she limped along. She was a good distance from her usual routes.

Jessie realized she was still wearing the plastic gloves. If someone saw her walking with the things on . . . She stripped them off and shoved them into the first trash Dumpster she passed. Art's spare key was in her pocket and posed another problem. Jessie hated to throw it away, but hanging on to it would be as stupid as Art's hanging on to his pictures of Laurie. Finally she decided to drop it down inside a concrete-block wall. It would stay there forever—or at least until the wall was knocked down.

Little by little her spirits rose, even as the aches in her legs grew worse. The call had been close, but she'd gotten away with it. Her left hand tightened on the strap of her camera case, now slung over her shoulder. Those photos disproved once and for all Art's version of his relationship with Laurie. Together with what Brenda had told her, they might even be enough to make Gutierrez take another look at his favorite football player.

Of course, that still left her with the problem of explaining just how she'd managed to *take* the pictures. Jessie stopped in the middle of the sidewalk as the full scope of the difficulty struck her. Breaking into someone else's apartment, even though she'd used a key and hadn't done any damage— She winced as she remembered the crash of the toilet tank behind her. Art's landlord would certainly complain about damages, and he'd have to replace the locks, and the key she'd dropped inside that wall. She'd better not tell the cops, after all—at least not right away.

Not until she'd figured out how to keep from getting arrested herself.

When she reached the apartment, she still hadn't figured out a solution to the problem, but by then she was more concerned about the spasms in her legs. At some point, either when she'd gone through the window or during her dive over that wall, she'd banged her shin. From the way her pants leg was sticking to her, it was clear that one of the scraped patches was oozing again. But this time she couldn't afford sympathy. When Val greeted her, Jessie answered as normally as she could and tried to keep from limping as she walked in. She didn't succeed entirely, and as she sat down on the couch with a secret sigh of relief, Val commented on her obvious condition.

"You're limping again," Val said. "I didn't expect you to go out, the way that leg was hurting you last night."

"I thought some exercise might help, so I went for

a walk." Jessie winced, not trying to cover it up this time. "I think I overdid it."

"Walking's probably not a bad idea," Val said. "Keep you from stiffening up." Jessie thought of her afternoon, diving out of windows and over fences, and suddenly had to choke back a laugh. She hadn't been stiff then, but it might be a different story in the morning.

Before Val could ask her any more questions, there was a knock, and Val went to answer the door. Jessie wasn't surprised to see Art and Randy—it was inevitable that they'd want to tell her and Val about the intruder. She admitted to herself that she really did want to know how things had looked from the other side of the locked door.

"How was your workout?" she asked, as though she hadn't noticed Art's limping.

"Art twisted his knee," Randy said. There was an interruption at that point as Val reacted—or overreacted in Jessie's opinion. For once, Art waved away the fallen-gladiator routine he usually welcomed.

"That was just the beginning," he said. "We got back to my place, and I was just starting to relax, when we heard a noise in the bathroom. Someone broke into the apartment."

"Who?" Val demanded at the same time Jessie asked, "Did you catch him?"

"I don't know who it was, but if I catch him, I'm going to collect damages out of his hide," Art said. His

145

fists clenched, and the ugly look was back on his face. "He just about wrecked the bathroom, and it's going to cost a couple hundred to fix things. Plus, the spare key's missing, so I'm going to have to get the landlord to change the locks, or I'll wake up and find the creep going through my wallet next time."

Randy took over, describing the locked door and the flood of water from the broken fixture. The story wavered between low comedy and cop show, as Randy told it. Jessie confined herself to exclamations and let Val ask most of the questions. Finally she asked the one Jessie had been itching to ask herself.

"Did you call the cops, sweetheart?" Val looked from one half-guilty face to the other. "You didn't, did you? Why not?"

"Hey, babe, it's not that big a deal," Art protested. "I mean, I'm pissed off at whoever it was, but it's not worth all the red tape. If he'd stolen my CD player or something, yeah, sure, then I'd call the cops, but we scared him off before he got anything. Like the cops are really going to bust their tails looking for some punk kid."

Jessie reacted along with Val, but she had expected this. Art wouldn't want to attract the attention of the police any more than he had to.

Both of the guys kept going over the story, adding fresh comments, while inside Jessie tension built to the screaming point. One thing she hadn't counted on was having to lie to Randy again. She hated it. And doing so was much harder than she had expected—harder than nerving herself to search an apartment illegally.

The subject finally exhausted itself, and the talk shifted to Jessie's bike. She told the guys the same modified truth she'd told Val, that a car had come too close and she'd fallen. Nothing about the car coming straight at her, nothing about the way it had lain in wait for her, nothing about the absence of headlights or the fact that it was stolen from an old woman who habitually left the key in the ignition. She didn't lie, but she told less than the full truth, and again it hurt to be keeping things from Randy. Jessie forced the feeling down and concentrated on watching Art.

Was it her imagination, or was there a hint of mockery on his face as she described the episode as a close call?

Randy came by in the morning to pick up the bicycle. Even with the backseat down, it barely fit into the hatchback, and he had to tie the rear door shut with a piece of rope. They dropped it off at the repair shop, where the manager shook his head over the bent wheel, warned of possible damage to the frame, and quoted a price that made Jessie wince. She'd have to call her folks and see if they could loan her some money; the repairs to the bike would wipe out the small bank account she'd built up working at Sweeny's. The rest of the day dragged, especially math, which had never been her favorite class. Instead of taking notes, she doodled while her mind wandered.

She still hadn't figured out a way to tell Gutierrez about the photos without getting into trouble. Mailing them anonymously wouldn't work; the detective knew she was a photographer, and he knew her suspicions about Art. She could lie and say she didn't know anything about them, but she doubted if he'd believe her. Besides, she'd had her fill of lying for a while. In the car that morning, Randy had been full of speculation about the break-in at Art's apartment. Keeping up her end of the conversation without letting the truth slip out or sounding unnatural had made her stomach knot with tension, and she'd changed the subject as quickly as possible. Sooner or later Jessie would have to tell him the truth, but she didn't dare until she'd gotten those pictures to Gutierrez. Which brought the circle of frustration back to the first question again: how could she get the photos to the detective?

That was one distraction. The other thing that turned the lecture into nothing but noise was a more subtle problem, but one that was potentially worse. Jessie was getting worried about Val. Her roommate sounded as sugary and happy with Art as ever. She'd fussed over him the night before; she defended Art against anything Jessie said and got angry when she said it. But underneath, it was obvious that something was wrong. Val's eyes had been red too often lately, and Jessie had caught a strange expression on her face the night before when Val had been looking at Art. She hadn't known she was being observed, and for a moment anger and hurt had vied on her face. And this morning Val had announced moodily that she was cutting classes. Valentine's Day was only two days away. Maybe Val had finally realized there wasn't going to be a diamond along with the heart-shaped balloons this time.

That was fine, as far as it went. Maybe she was callous, but Jessie figured it was about time for Val to wake up. She'd been building a very fancy castle in the air, with herself in the starring role as fairy princess. If the castle had fallen apart, great, but Jessie didn't expect it to collapse quietly. She was afraid Val would try to put pressure on Art. And that could be very dangerous.

The class finally ended. She'd have to borrow someone's notes later to find out what the instructor had actually said; the few notes she'd made were illegible. At least her legs felt better today, and she was on the west side of campus. It wasn't far to Sweeny's.

When she went to get the film out of her case, she noticed something that crystallized the day's fears. Her lens cap was missing, the one she'd replaced after she'd lost the original on the street two nights before. It wasn't the lens cap that bothered her; they were cheap, and she'd lost a dozen over the years. But where had she lost this one? She was afraid she knew.

She'd set her camera down for a moment in Art's bedroom when she was going through the books. Only a few minutes later, Art and Randy had gotten there, and she'd put the camera away while hiding in the bathroom. She was almost positive the lens cap *hadn't* been on the camera when she'd put it in the case. Which meant it had gotten lost in Art's bedroom.

He wouldn't need fingerprints to know whose lens cap it was, and by extension, who'd been in his apartment. If he found it. At that thought, Jessie's spirits lifted. From the state of that bedroom, she figured Art hadn't cleaned it in weeks, and it might be several more before he got around to it. In the welter of clothes and books and athletic shoes, something as small as a lens cap would be almost invisible. She was probably still safe. But the realization of her carelessness left her shaken.

She got busy, transcribing old records onto the computer for Mr. Sweeny. It was an ongoing job that would take months to complete, and it demanded enough of her attention that for a while she could bury herself in the work without having to worry about murders or roommates. Jessie was surprised when Jack broke her concentration.

"Jessie?" he said. He was standing beside her and obviously had been for several minutes before she'd noticed. "I said I'm ready to leave now. Go ahead and shut down the computer and let's lock up."

"Lock up?" she repeated blankly. She looked up at

the clock. Somehow it was seven o'clock already. "But I've got some film I wanted to develop. You go on, I'll lock up as soon as I'm done." As she spoke, she realized suddenly how tired she felt, and how hungry. The last few days had been rough.

"I'm not so sure that's a good idea," he said, frowning. "I'd planned on giving you a ride home. After what happened the last time you worked late . . ."

"Believe me, I haven't forgotten it," she assured him. "Don't worry, I won't walk home by myself. I'm too tired to, anyway. I'll call Randy and have him pick me up."

"Well—look, if he's not there, either call a cab or you can call me at home. Just don't go out alone."

"I won't," she promised. After repeating his warning, Mr. Sweeny left, and Jessie headed into the darkroom to develop the film.

Most of the pictures had turned out well. Besides close-ups that showed Art's photos in detail, she'd taken several from a few steps back, showing not only the photos, but their position in Art's bedroom. She made enlargements of a few of them, including the steamy kiss and a shot of the photo album open on Art's bedroom floor. Now all she had to do was figure out where to keep them. Her work file at home wasn't safe, that was obvious. She'd always been careful to keep her work separate from the studio's, but she didn't have much choice. The dummy envelope labeled "ART" had been on her desk for well over a week now, undisturbed. The pictures would be safer there.

She had just finished putting the prints and negatives in separate envelopes when a cold draft stirred a stack of photos on the counter and knocked a few onto the floor. Jessie bent to pick them up. She stopped, still half-stooped, as she looked up and realized where the breeze had come from. The door to the darkroom was open, and Art Ducas stood in it, blocking her way out.

"Hi, Art," she said, trying for a casual tone. Despite her best efforts, there was a quiver in her voice, but she went on as though it were perfectly normal for him to be there at this time of the night with that enraged look on his face. "I didn't hear you come in. You surprised me, I thought I locked the door."

As she spoke, she was trying desperately to remember. *Had* she locked the front door? She didn't think so. It was the type that locked automatically when a little lever was pressed. Jessie couldn't remember doing so herself, and she didn't think Mr. Sweeny had on his way out. And the bell on the door was broken. Jack had been saying for two months that he had to get it fixed, but he hadn't done so. Jessie wished he had; this was twice Art had been able to sneak up on her.

"Where's Val?"

"Val?" His question caught her off guard. "I don't know, home, I guess. I haven't been there since this morning. Why?" As Jessie spoke, she remembered Val's announcement that morning that she was tired of school. Maybe what she'd meant was she was tired of Art. If Val had split, Jessie didn't blame her.

"I've been looking for her all afternoon," he said. He looked as though he was barely hanging on to his temper, but he hadn't lost it yet. "We need to get some things straight."

"Well, I haven't seen her," Jessie said. Despite his anger, she relaxed slightly. If he was searching for Val, he might not bother with her. She was acutely aware of the photos only a few feet from Art's elbow, pictures that would provoke a roar of anger if he saw them. And possibly a much more dangerous reaction.

"Damn!" He was swearing more to himself than at her, and she relaxed further. But his next words caused her to tense up again. "She'd better not—I found something she'd better be able to explain."

Found something. Jessie's thoughts leapt to the lens cap, and she stiffened. Slight as the reaction was, he noticed it. "What do you know about it?" he snarled.

"Know about what?" she asked, thinking as the words came out that her voice was wrong, the words were wrong, she sounded guilty. She got a grip on herself, but it was too late.

He took a step into the small room. "About that break-in at my apartment," he said. His face was twisting once more into the expression of rage she'd seen so often, but it had never terrified her the way it did now. Her chest felt paralyzed, as though it didn't intend ever to draw another breath. And if she didn't get out of here, she might not.

"The one last night?" Her voice sounded shrill in her own ears, and she fought to control it.

"How many do you think there've been?" he said through clenched teeth.

"I don't know," she said. It was a stupid thing to say, but it was all Jessie could think of.

"You know more than you're saying, that's for sure. Now tell me what it is." He seemed bigger than ever in the narrow space between the counters.

She took a step backward, and he took another toward her. It was like a dance, she thought, a very dangerous dance, but it couldn't last long. The far wall was only a few feet behind her.

"I don't know what you're talking about," she said. He took another step. The door was clear if she could get around him, but she'd never make it. The room wasn't that big, and she'd seen Art move on the football field. For all his size and bulk, he moved with the speed of a striking snake.

"Damn you, answer me," he said. His voice was thick, and his face darkened as he took another step forward. In another moment he would explode. His right hand reached toward Jessie, and she shrank back. She knew the damage those hands could inflict. If he touched her, she was convinced, he'd kill her.

154

She bumped against the counter as they took another step in their deadly dance, and her hand fell on a metal-foil envelope. Fixer. It was the chemical used to stop the developing process. Jessie picked it up, her eyes never leaving Art as he took another step forward. In a single movement she ripped the top open, then brought her hand up suddenly, dashing the contents of the envelope into Art's eyes.

He let out a roar and grabbed for her, but the harsh chemicals transformed his face into a mask of tears and whitish powder, and he stumbled, unable to see her as she dodged around him and out the door to freedom.

Behind her, Art yelled again in pain and frustration. "Jessie! Come back here—I can't *see*—help me. . . ."

She snatched up her camera bag and ran out the front door. Art stumbled out of the darkroom as she fled, blinking frantically against the tears streaming down his face. His hands pawed at his eyes; then with another curse he turned and lurched back into the darkroom. The stainless-steel lab sink was the closest source of water.

Jessie didn't bother closing the door—she just ran. Art's eyes would be okay as long as he rinsed them, and he was probably doing that right now. But they'd look pretty bad for several days, and she knew how much they must hurt. She'd gotten some fixer powder in her own eye once, and it had felt like fire. He'd already been in a murderous rage; Jessie didn't want to think about what would happen if he caught up with her now.

She ran down the street, ignoring the people who stared as she passed. After a block or so, she slowed down. She didn't dare go home yet. That would be the first place he'd look, once he could see well enough to drive. At the next corner she turned toward campus instead of her apartment.

Although the sun had set several hours earlier, it was still early evening, and many of the restaurants and shops near campus were open. Jessie kept an eye out for Art's Mustang, but as long as she stayed where there were plenty of people, she should be all right. She dug in the side pouch of her camera case for change. Nothing. Belatedly she recalled spending the last of her loose change on a soda between classes that afternoon.

At least her much abused legs weren't aching this time. They'd gone through a toughening-up in the last week that would impress even the football coach. Jessie went into a small café and asked to use the phone but was curtly refused. She bit her lip; she didn't have her credit cards or checkbook with her, either.

There was a pay phone outside a convenience store in the next block, and Jessie wondered if she could borrow a quarter from the cashier. It wasn't necessary—when she checked the coin return, she found a quarter that someone had ignored. Hurriedly she dialed

Randy's number, then listened to it ring. And ring.

C'mon, answer. She was almost ready to give up when Randy answered, out of breath.

"Randy, thank God," Jessie said, sagging against the phone as relief at hearing his voice washed over her.

"Jessie? What's wrong?"

"I'll explain when you get here, but could you come pick me up?" Before he could respond, she added, "I'm not at home, I'm down at the convenience store across from the life-sciences building. Could you come right away?"

There was silence on the other end of the line for a moment. "Jessie, I'm standing here dripping soapsuds on the rug. I was in the shower. Are you all right, or can it wait a few minutes?"

"I'm all right now, but I had a run-in with Art down at the studio, and I'm afraid he's looking for me."

Randy uttered a couple of swear words and said, "All right, just give me five minutes to rinse off and get dressed. You stay put." There was a click as he hung up without saying good-bye.

Jessie replaced the receiver and shut her eyes for a moment, feeling gratitude to her unknown benefactor who had left a quarter in the return slot. Then she stepped over in front of the big plate-glass windows lining the front of the store. If Art came by, she could duck inside quickly, and she'd be able to spot Randy as soon as he came.

It wasn't much more than the promised five minutes before Randy's white Toyota pulled up in front of the convenience store. Jessie was around the side and pulling the door open even before he had a chance to turn off the engine. She sank back against the upholstery with a sigh of relief.

Randy left the motor idling and asked, "All right, Jessie, what happened?" His hair was still damp from the shower, and he smelled like soap. As far as Jessie was concerned, he was the most gorgeous thing she'd ever seen. Briefly, she told him what had happened, starting with Art's appearance in the door of the darkroom. Randy whistled when she described how she'd thrown the fixer in his eyes.

"Man, he *would* have killed you if he'd gotten hold of you then, no joke. But why'd he think Val or you had anything to do with that mess at his place?"

"I don't know about Val, but . . ." Jessie hesitated, then plunged into a description of the way in which she'd broken into Art's apartment the previous day. When she finished, Randy seemed torn between amusement and outrage.

"Do you know what a mess you made in that john?" he demanded. He grinned. "And those were Art's new shoes that got soaked. Between them and the damage deposit—he can kiss *that* good-bye—I don't blame Art for being just a little upset, do you?" His grin faded. "But I can't believe you actually did that, Jessie. That's pretty raw, breaking into someone's place and snooping like that."

"I know, but I *had* to!" she said desperately. "And I was right; that photo album showed he had a lot more going with Laurie than he ever admitted to you *or* the cops. I'm convinced Brenda was telling the truth, about Laurie and about the steroids, but I'm afraid to go back and look for proof now." In a much lower voice, she went on. "I'm sorry I lied to you. I couldn't think what else to do."

"It just makes me feel like an idiot, telling you the whole story when you were on the other side of that door," Randy said. He shifted into reverse and backed out.

Jessie didn't say anything as they pulled out onto the street. He was right, but there wasn't any way she could go back and change things now. They waited through a light, then he asked, "Where do you want to go?"

"I'd better go back to the studio first," she said. "Even if he's still there, I don't think he'll do anything if you're with me, and I have to lock up."

"I hope he is there," Randy said grimly. "I can't blame him for being mad about his apartment, but I'm beginning to think you're right about one thing. Art's involved somehow, and I don't like him threatening you."

At last, she thought, *someone believes me*.

"Don't forget the steroids," she said quietly. "Those were what I was really looking for in his apartment."

"Everyone always accuses us of steroids," Randy growled. "You know what I think about that."

"But if he thought Brenda was going to ruin his career, and if Laurie was pushing him harder than Val . . ."

"I'm not convinced he's a murderer," he said stubbornly, and Jessie almost screamed. "But involved, yeah. Thing is, I just can't see him doing it deliberately. You tell me Art's gone crazy-mad and killed somebody by accident—yeah, that I'll believe. Maybe he's even on steroids, although I didn't think he was that stupid. But commit cold-blooded murder? No way."

"Well, someone killed Laurie," Jessie said. "And Brenda. And Art's the only one I know of who's been threatening people."

They pulled up in front of Sweeny's. The door was shut, but the lights were on inside. "I can't tell if he's in there," Jessie said. She was nervous about going in, even with Randy.

"We won't find out sitting here," he said, getting out. He stared at the door, hands on hips, while she got out. "Anyway, I want to see those pictures you took."

The first thing Jessie did when they got inside was to flip the lever so the door would lock automatically. The silence told them the studio was deserted, but nevertheless, they called hello and checked each room. The gallery, the back room, the tiny bathroom wedged in a corner—the place was empty. The last room they checked was the darkroom. Here there were signs of Art's struggle. White fixer powder had made a mess all over the floor, and the empty envelope was in the middle of it. The tap in the work sink was dripping, and the countertop was flooded. More water was on the floor, along with a wad of used paper towels. Jessie was relieved; Art must have washed the fixer off. Her reaction might be irrational, since she was trying to prove he was a murderer, but she was glad he'd taken care of his eyes. She hadn't meant to blind him; she just wanted to get away.

"Jeesh, he left a mess," Randy said, trying to mop up water and fixer powder with more paper towels. "Guess it's fair, considering what you did in his bathroom. . . . You need to get anything before we lock up and get out of here?"

"My pictures," Jessie said, and stopped. She didn't even need to look to know they were missing. Just before Art had walked in, she'd put the prints and negatives in a couple of envelopes. They should have still been on the counter. But they were gone.

Quickly she checked through all the prints and negatives in the darkroom, but it was no use. Once more the photos she'd counted on for proof had been taken. A sudden thought hit her, and she ran out to her desk. The flimsy drawer had been forced open, and the junk inside looked as though it had been tossed like a salad. The unmarked envelope with the pictures of Art and Misty was gone. On top of the desk, the dummy envelope marked "ART" had been ripped open. The photos of the student art show had been ripped in half.

"Jessie?" Randy came up behind her as she stood looking down at the mess.

"He's got them. Every photo I've taken that might, *might* have convinced Gutierrez at least to ask some questions! Every one of them is gone." Jessie turned away, defeated. "Forget it. I'll have to call Mr. Sweeny in the morning and explain the mess, but I'm too tired to bother with it now. What's the use, anyway? Art's got the pictures."

She went through the studio, turning off the lights, and made sure the back door was bolted, then double-checked the front door when they were out. Randy said nothing until they were back in the car. Then he asked her, "Do you want to go to the cops? He did threaten you."

"I can see me trying to explain this to Gutierrez." Her voice took on a mocking singsong. "You say Mr. Ducas threatened you? Why? Oh, because you broke into his apartment? And so you blinded him with chemicals?" Her voice abruptly returned to normal. "I can't think of any way to tell them that won't get me into more trouble than Art. Let's just go back to the apartment."

She feared what they might find at the apartment. Art might be waiting for her, seeking vengeance for his eyes. Or worse, what if Val had finally come home and he'd caught up with her? But the Mustang wasn't parked out front, and the apartment was quiet and undisturbed. Jessie relaxed into the arm Randy had draped around her shoulder. For a while at least, the excitement was over.

"Isn't Val here?" Randy asked, looking around.

That roused Jessie again. She went through the apartment rapidly, as she had the studio. The place was deserted. Val's clothes were still in her room, and she hadn't left a note on the refrigerator door, their normal message center. Jessie felt a pang as she noticed how much of Art's stuff was scattered around. But there was nothing missing. The apartment looked just the way it had when Jessie had left for class that morning, hours ago.

"I don't know where she is," Jessie said. Her voice sounded as weary as she felt. "I'm just going to go to bed. Maybe in the morning I'll wake up, and it will all be just a bad dream."

"I'll make sure no one wakes you up before then with another nightmare," Randy said. Jessie felt her mouth fall open stupidly and tried to shut it, but the motion triggered a huge yawn. She blinked at him as soon as she could shut her mouth.

"I'm sleeping right there," he said, pointing to the couch. "Just in case Art decides to come ask you some more questions. Got a spare pillow?"

The next morning they were at the studio cleaning

up by the time Mr. Sweeny got there. They'd stayed up talking a while longer until Jessie couldn't keep her eyes open; but Art never came, and the night had passed quietly. More troubling was the fact that Val had never returned to the apartment. By the time they'd left that morning, there'd still been no word from her.

The cleanup had uncovered one good thing: Art had overlooked one photograph. Jessie had forgotten about it herself; she'd left one negative in the enlarger. It was one of the best, showing the open album, amid the clutter of Art's bedroom, displaying the almost R-rated embrace. Unfortunately, the rest of the negatives were gone, along with the photos.

"All it proves is that he lied about Laurie," Jessie said, studying the photo in the cold light of day. She'd printed a fresh copy. It was a cold light in more than one sense; Tucson was having one of its rare gray days, and there was a chance of snow before nightfall. Mid-February was still winter, even in the Southwest.

"That's all you need to prove," Randy said. Jessie was discouraged, and he seemed determined to keep up her spirits. "All you want is to get the cops to ask him questions, right? Let them worry about it after that. If he's really a threat to Val, they'll stop him."

"If she isn't dead already," Jessie muttered under her breath. Art had been looking for Val the day before, and by this time he might have found her.

Explaining the mess to Mr. Sweeny was difficult.

166

His immediate reaction was to call the police, and it took both Jessie's and Randy's best arguments to dissuade him. Jessie found herself once more explaining about her unauthorized visit to Art's apartment, and from the look on Jack's face, she knew there was no use trying to persuade him not to tell her father the next time they got together. All she could hope was that things would be settled by then, with Art in jail for murder.

That thought stayed with her through the morning, as did Randy. Since it was Saturday, they had no classes, and he hung around while she finished the cleanup at the studio, then took her out to lunch. They stopped back by the apartment after that, and there was a note on the refrigerator from Val.

"Thank heavens!" Jessie exclaimed when she spotted it. Her enthusiasm faded as she read the brief note. *Jessie—you may have been right. Art called yesterday, and I'm frightened. I have to think things out. See you later. Val.* That was all there was.

"'You may have been right,'" Randy echoed, reading over Jessie's shoulder. "Right about what?"

"About Art and the fact that he could be dangerous." She took the note off the door and read through it again. "Damn, this doesn't really say anything. Where *is* she?"

"Offhand, I'd say she's someplace trying to decide if it's time to cut her losses," Randy said. "It sounds like she's at least figured out she's not going to get that ring she was counting on. If she knows anything about Art that she hasn't been saying . . ."

"It's possible," Jessie said. She weighed it in her mind. Val had been sure Art was going to marry her, but would that have been enough to make her cover for him if he was a murderer? Reluctantly, Jessie came to the conclusion it would. Val had made it clear, time after time, that Art came before anything else. Art, and her future with Art. Now that there was no future there, what would she do?

They stayed at the apartment all afternoon, but Val never showed up. Around two the phone rang, and Jessie dived for it. Snatching it up, she said, "Hello?" hoping to hear her roommate's voice.

"Is she there?" Art's peremptory demand was a relief. If he was still searching for Val, she had to be all right.

"I haven't seen her all day," Jessie replied truthfully.

"What the hell were you trying to do last night, Jessie, blind me? If you thought that was funny . . ."

She pulled the phone away from her ear and wordlessly extended it to Randy, who took it with a look of grim satisfaction. Before Art could get any further with his diatribe, Randy cut him off.

"Yo, *Ducas*!"

"Randy?" Jessie could hear Art's voice clearly, and Randy moved the phone a half inch farther from his ear. "Did that crazy girlfriend of yours tell you what she *did* to me? Man, she damn near blinded me."

"She told me." Randy's voice was as grim as his face. "She also told me about the way you threatened her. Again, Art. I told you to lay off. And it sounds to me like she's been asking you some good questions."

"C'mon, Beckman, she's crazy jealous or something." Art's volume dropped suddenly, leaving Jessie with only Randy's end of the conversation.

There was silence for a moment as he listened; then Randy said, "I don't know either. But there're two girls dead, and you keep pretending you don't know anything about either of them, and you keep threatening Jessie and Val. And you wonder *why* you need to answer some questions?"

Art said something else, but this time Jessie could barely hear the rumble of his words. Then Randy said, "I have no idea where Val is, and right now I don't care. All I know is, you'd better not try leaning on Jessie again, man, because I'll take you apart if you try it!" He hung up and smiled at Jessie. "I think maybe I convinced him."

"You convinced me," she said with her own smile. A worried look replaced it as she added, "I wish Val would call."

But the phone remained silent after that. Late that evening they went out for a bite to eat, and Randy stopped at a shopping center on impulse. "Wait here," he told her, then disappeared into a grocery store. When he returned ten minutes later, he had a big heart-shaped box of chocolates.

"Happy Valentine's Day, sweetheart," he said, leaning in the passenger's door to kiss her.

She returned the kiss, but when he got back in and started the car, she said, "Don't call me that, please."

"What?"

"Sweetheart," Jessie said with a shiver. "That's what Val always calls Art, and every time I hear that word, I'm going to remember this month." She paused, looking at the blackness out the window. "It'll be Valentine's Day in a few hours. She thought she was going to be getting a diamond."

Val wasn't at the apartment when they got there. Jessie ate a few of the chocolates, but she wasn't in the mood for candy.

They were discussing whether or not Randy should spend another night on the couch when the door opened and Val walked in. "Val! Where have you *been?*" Jessie demanded, rushing over and giving her a fierce hug. "I've been worried."

"I'm sorry you were upset," Val said. She looked exhausted—not just tired, but drained of all response and emotion. "Art broke up with me yesterday, and we had a—a fight, I guess you'd call it. I had to figure out what to do."

"Sit down," Jessie urged. She pulled Val over to the couch and gently shoved her down onto it. "Now, why don't you just start at the beginning and tell us everything?"

"He came over yesterday morning, after Randy picked you up," Val began obediently. "His knee was still swollen from when he twisted it at weights, and I told him he ought to go see the trainer. He wouldn't, and when I tried to make him, he blew up and told me he was afraid to, that he's been having a lot of trouble with that knee, and he was afraid the trainer would say he couldn't play pro ball."

"God," Randy breathed, "that'd kill Art." Jessie tried to remember more than her own fears the night before. Art *had* been favoring that leg when they did their deadly little dance in the darkroom, before she'd thrown the fixer at him.

"I told him that he couldn't just throw his career away like that, he *had* to go see the doctor," Val went on. "And he accused me of—he said all I was interested in was money." She bit her lip. Jessie said nothing, but as sorry as she felt for Val, there was at least some truth to the accusation. Art's career in the pros had always figured large in Val's dreams for the future.

"And I was right, wasn't I?"

Art stood in the door, his face bitter. For the first time Jessie noticed how he was standing, all his weight on his left leg. His right pants leg looked tight around his knee. Randy said something Jessie didn't catch as Art took a step forward. His eyes were fixed on Val, and rage was twisting his face into the familiar mask Jessie had seen before.

"You going to tell them the rest, or shall I?" He

171

limped forward another step. "Going to tell them the way you lied, and set people up, and—"

"Art, *no!*" Val screamed, scrambling off the couch as Art made a sudden rush at her, almost falling as his weak knee gave way. Randy grabbed for him, and Art twisted with startling speed, pushing him back.

"She's not going to get away with it," Art panted, swinging at Randy. Randy backed away from the blow, while Jessie grabbed Val's arm and pulled her away from the couch. The cord of the telephone caught around her foot, and she pulled it off the table, sending it crashing to the floor. The noise of the bell as it broke was lost in the crash as the coffee table, shoved violently aside, went over, one leg snapping off. Art feigned again in Randy's direction, then threw himself toward the two girls in a clumsy tackle.

"She's not getting away with it!" he roared as he grabbed for Val. Val screamed, the sound choking off as Art's hands fastened on her throat for a moment before Randy grabbed him from behind. He tore Art's hands loose, and Jessie pushed Val behind her.

Art heaved his massive shoulders like a bull shrugging off a fly, and his left elbow shot back, catching Randy in the pit of the stomach. Randy's grasp faltered and Art broke free again, reaching beyond Jessie for Val. Jessie tried to block him with her arms, terrified by his blind fury.

Randy grabbed Art's arm from behind and swung Art around to face him. As he came around, Randy's right fist connected with Art's chin with a solid *crack*.

For an instant everything froze. Then Art's eyes rolled back in his head, and he collapsed in what seemed like slow motion.

"Wow," Randy said. He stretched out his left hand to Jessie and pulled her to her feet. "Man, I didn't expect that." He rubbed his right hand, wincing. "Same damned finger I broke during the season." His hand was starting to swell already.

"He was going to kill me," Val said in a tiny voice that didn't even sound like hers. "He really was."

"Yeah, I got that impression," Randy said.

Jessie picked up the wreckage of the phone. "We can't call the cops on this." There was no dial tone.

"The cops?" Val still didn't sound like herself, and Jessie spoke roughly, hoping to shake her back to reality.

"Yeah, the cops. This time Gutierrez is going to listen—I don't care what sort of phony alibi Art has. You're going to tell the truth yourself this time, Val. You knew all along about the steroids, didn't you?" Jessie waited until Val had given her a hesitant nod, then went on. "What else did you know? No, never mind, you might as well just tell the cops. But this time we're going to get the whole story."

"What was Art talking about, anyway?" Randy put in. "All that stuff about you weren't going to get away with it?"

Instead of answering, Val started to shake violently.

173

"Shock," Jessie muttered. "Val, can I get you any-thing? Do you need to lie down?"

Val shook her head wordlessly and stumbled off toward the kitchen. A moment later Jessie heard the water running. On the floor by her feet, Art let out a groan and stirred slightly, then slipped back into unconsciousness.

"Maybe we'd better get him over to the emergency room and call the cops from there," Jessie suggested. "Look at his knee." Art's right knee was straining the fabric of his jeans.

"We can't get him into the hatchback," Randy muttered. "Not unless we lay him down in the back, and he's too tall. He couldn't have walked very far with that leg. Let me go see if I can find the Mustang."

He went out, leaving the door open, as Val came back into the room, her face damp from rinsing it. Jessie, her eyes still on Art, said, "I tried to tell you a long time ago he was dangerous, but you wouldn't listen."

Val came over and stood beside Jessie. Looking down at Art, she said, "I hate him." Her voice was soft, intense, and bitter. "Did you know it's Valentine's Day?" Jessie glanced at the clock, surprised. It was a few minutes after midnight. Val was right—February 14 had begun.

"Yeah, you thought you'd be getting a ring this time," Jessie said, glancing sideways at her roommate. Val's face was twisted into a mask of hate in much the same way Art's had been earlier. "Instead of just . . ." Val's long bead earring caught the light and finally triggered the vagrant memory that had been bothering Jessie since she'd found Brenda's body. "Earrings! That was what I saw, that red bead earring Art gave you for Christmas! It looked just like the pyracantha berries and the drops of blood. It was caught in Brenda's hair. It must have been knocked off by a paramedic when they moved her. Gutierrez was right, walk all over the evidence . . ."

"So that was where I lost it," Val whispered. For a moment, the words made no sense to Jessie.

"Val, what do you mean?" she began, then stopped in horror as her roommate smiled at her, a hideous expression, completely mad.

"I'm sorry you remembered that," Val said, still talking softly. "But it doesn't make any difference." She took a step closer to Jessie and brought up her hand. In it was Art's hunting knife that had been missing for weeks. Jessie's breath caught. The blade gleamed in the light.

"When Art started talking, it would have been all over, anyway," Val said. Her voice was still quiet, but there was a note of steel in it harder and sharper than the knife she was now pressing against Jessie's ribs. "This way I still have a chance." She crowded up against Jessie, making it look as though she were leaning on her, and said calmly, "Randy's going to put Art in his car, and we're going to go for a little

175

drive. Just you and me and Art."

"You're crazy," Jessie managed to say, before she felt the tip of the needle-sharp knife pressing through her sweater.

"I think maybe I am," Val said. "I must have been to think Art cared about me." She smiled, the same hellish smile as before. "But Art's going to be the one who pays for it."

The knife point dug in a little more, and Jessie could feel a trickle of blood rolling down her side. "You try to warn Randy, and he'll never move fast enough to keep me from killing you," Val whispered fiercely, just as Randy walked back through the door.

"Art's Mustang was parked on the next block. I moved it around front," Randy announced. He came over to Jessie and Val. If he noticed the way they were standing, he didn't give any indication; he was watching Art. "He given you any more trouble?"

Jessie couldn't answer. She was having trouble breathing. Val's answer came coolly. "He's still out, but I think we'd better get him in the car."

"Before he comes to. Good idea." Randy bent over and hoisted Art's deadweight up to a sitting position, then got him draped over his shoulder in a fireman's hold. He straightened up, grunting. "God, he weighs a ton. Help me get him in the front seat, Jessie." He carried Art out, maneuvering awkwardly through the door.

Jessie felt a tiny flare of pain as Val pressed the

knife harder against Jessie's back. "Go on," she whispered, "and remember. No signal." Jessie went toward the door, Val's arm around her waist. Anyone looking at them casually would have thought Val was holding on to Jessie for support. Not holding a knife to her back.

They reached the Mustang a step behind Randy, who stood back to let Jessie open the passenger's door for him. At a prompt from the knife, she did so. Val pulled her back, renewing the pressure of the sharp point, as Randy, grunting, managed to dump Art into the bucket seat. There was a dull thud as Art flopped sideways, his head hitting the door, and almost toppled out of the car before Randy caught him and pushed him back in place.

"Hope he hasn't got a concussion," Randy said, fastening the seat belt around Art to hold him in place. "He needs to be able to answer questions."

"Maybe we'd better pack some ice on that knee," Val said. She sounded concerned. "It looks awful."

"It's not that far to the hospital."

"That sounds like a good idea," Jessie said, prompted by the knife. She managed to keep her voice steady. "Your hand needs some, too. There's a bag in the freezer."

"Can't hurt, I guess. Clobber him if he wakes up and gives you any trouble. I still can't believe Art Ducas is a murderer." Randy headed back toward the apartment.

As soon as he left, Val released Jessie's arm and stepped to the open car door. Before Jessie could draw a breath to yell, the knife was pressed against Art's throat. "One sound and he's dead," Val said. She motioned with her head. "Go around and get in, we're leaving. *Move!*" Jessie hurried around the car, while Val forced her way into the backseat. Jessie pulled the driver's door open and slid behind the wheel, as Val leaned forward between the bucket seats, holding the blade to Art's throat. Art lolled against the seat belt.

"Start the car," Val said. Jessie fumbled for a moment with the unfamiliar gears, and Val added, "Dammit, get *going!*" A thin line of red appeared on Art's throat as the razor-sharp edge broke the skin, and Jessie hurried to turn the key. The Mustang started with its familiar roar, and jerked as Jessie let the clutch out too abruptly.

"Do that again, and you'll be the one who gets the knife," Val snapped. She settled herself halfway between the seats on the console and shifted the point of the blade so it was pressed firmly against Jessie's ribs. "Turn left at the next block. I want to make sure Randy isn't following us." Jessie followed her instructions, moving away from the first direction Randy would check, the route to the university hospital. After several turns down side streets and one alley, Val had Jessie turn west on Speedway.

"Faster," she said tersely. Jessie stepped on the gas, but within a couple of blocks she slacked off again, as gradually as she could. No matter what Val had in mind, Jessie was sure she wasn't going to like it. The longer it took to get wherever they were going, the better.

Jessie slowed still further as they approached I-10 and glanced sideways questioningly. "Keep going," Val said, underlining the command with another nudge from the knife. They passed under the interstate, heading toward Gates Pass and the road to the Desert Museum. Past the interstate there were fewer houses and more open country.

"You killed Laurie, didn't you?" Jessie asked quietly.

"Just drive," Val said. Beside Jessie in the front seat, Art groaned and thrashed about briefly before subsiding again. Jessie stole a quick peek at him. It looked as though he was coming to. She stared at the road, as a few large splats appeared on the windshield. A mix of rain and snow was starting to fall, and she could feel the slickness under the tires as she braked for a red light.

"Val, at least I want to know why," she said, adding mentally, *since you're going to kill me.* She didn't want to put the thought into words. "Was it because Laurie was dating Art?"

"She was going to ruin everything," Val snarled. "I should have realized how stupid Art was, letting her find out about the drugs—I should have just let her have him."

"Steroids," Jessie said quietly. "Brenda was right."

It all fit so perfectly, now that she was looking at it from the right direction. Somehow Laurie had found out about Art's use of steroids and had tried to use that knowledge as a lever to make Art break up with Val. Instead, Val had found out and killed her, protecting Art's secret and her own hold on him. And Brenda—she'd known about Laurie and Art, she'd known about the steroids. Obviously, she hadn't figured out that Val was the murderer. It would have been easy for Val to slip out that morning and join Brenda on her jog. When Jessie found the body, Val had already been in the shower. She must have waited in her bedroom until Jessie had left, then gone in to wash off the blood. There would have been blood on her, Jessie thought. There had been blood all over. Drops of blood that looked like berries, or like Val's red bead earring.

But there were still parts that didn't make sense. Jessie let her foot ease on the accelerator as the road swooped toward the mountains. The rain-snow combination was still falling lightly, and it was getting more slippery. The light was red at the Greasewood intersection, and when it changed and they started forward, the tires spun for a moment before gripping the pavement. The road started to climb steeply.

"So Art was innocent all along," Jessie said.

"Don't be stupid," Val interrupted. "He figured it out, he just didn't say anything. Too scared he'd lose his career."

"S'lie." Jessie's grip on the wheel tightened as Art spoke for the first time. His voice was slurred but gaining strength. "Tha's a lie. Didn't—know. Just thought maybe, and when I tried to get ridda . . . get rid of the . . ."

"Shut *up*!" Val yelled at him. Abruptly, she lashed across with her right hand, slamming her fist down on his swollen knee. Art screamed, a throat-tearing sound. Val had the knife against Jessie's ribs again before she had time to react or take advantage of the distraction. It had been too sudden.

"Art, don't try anything," Val said. Her voice was once more under tight control. Art didn't say anything, just continued to make little gasping noises of pain. "Unless you want Jessie driving with a knife in her. Faster, Jessie."

"I can't," Jessie said. The icy road was more terrifying than the knife. Speedway had turned into Gates Pass Road, and they were almost to the end of the houses. "I *can't*." Jessie could feel blood trickling down her side again as Val increased the pressure, but she slowed anyway as a closely spaced series of yellow warning signs with chevrons loomed ahead of them, indicating a left-hand curve. Val gripped the back of Jessie's seat with her free hand, shifting herself forward on the console so she was riding between Jessie and Art.

"You'd better not slow down again," Val warned her.

"Why?" Jessie kept her attention on the road, trying to ignore the point still digging into her side. "You're just going to kill us anyway, aren't you?"

Behind and below her, Jessie saw a flash of headlights as another car came through the Greasewood intersection on a red light. Whoever it was, was going fast. *Randy?* It might be, if he'd spotted the Mustang on Speedway. Jessie tried to watch for the headlights in the rearview mirror. They passed the sign welcoming them to Tucson Mountain Park.

"I didn't intend to," Val said. "But nothing worked out the way it was supposed to."

"Didn' *know* she killed Laurie, but I thought . . . least Laurie wouldn' tell coach about the pills." Art's voice was still slurred, whether from pain or concussion, Jessie couldn't tell. "After Brenda . . . then I knew. Tol' her I knew. Didn' wan' to marry a murderer. Didn' wan' to marry her anyway. . . ."

"You did," Val said. Jessie thought wildly, *After everything that's happened, that's the first time Val's sounded really murderous.* "At first you did." Tears of pure rage slid down her cheeks unheeded.

"Crazy . . ." Art's voice trailed off into silence again and he sagged against the seat belt. Jessie tried to bite back a sob. He was unconscious again, she thought, leaving her alone with her murdering roommate.

"There's a turnoff just this side of the pass. Pull off the road there," Val directed.

The light rain and snow had stopped falling, but

the road was still slick from it. The narrow, winding mountain road didn't bother Jessie in daylight with dry pavement, but on a night like this it was treacherous.

"That was what your fights were about," Jessie said, as the last puzzle pieces dropped into place. "Art had guessed, and he didn't want any part of it."

"He's not as innocent as he wants you to think," Val said, biting off the words. "He didn't want to say anything to the cops, for fear they'd find out about the steroids."

Jessie had already figured that out. If Art had been willing to risk his career, Brenda might have lived, and she wouldn't be driving over Gates Pass in the middle of the night with a killer poking holes in her ribs. She checked the rearview mirror again. There was no sign of the headlights she'd seen earlier, but there was a wedge of Tucson visible in the notch formed by the canyon. It was a misty carpet of lights far in the distance. They had almost reached the top of the pass and the turnoff to the picnic area. It would be closed at this hour, but she'd be able to pull off the road. Then what?

"Why did you leave Brenda in front of the apartment?" Jessie asked. "Did you want me to find her?"

"That wasn't supposed to happen either," Val said bitterly. "If you hadn't found her, you might not have gotten so involved. Although, I don't know—maybe it would have turned out this way no matter what. You wouldn't leave anything alone, you kept pushing. I wanted to warn Art, not you."

"What about that note?"

"What note?" Val asked. Jessie didn't answer. Art must have slipped that into her book—he knew Val was guilty and had been afraid to come forward, so he'd tried to warn her off. She thought about the sensation she'd had of being watched, the phone calls with no one there, all the little warnings, and wondered which had been Val, which Art, and which her own imagination. She wouldn't have much time to wonder about it.

"You were the one in the car that night, weren't you?" Jessie asked, her eyes straying to the rearview mirror. There were no headlights visible behind them on the twisty road.

"I wasn't trying to hit you," Val said. It almost sounded like apology. "But you'd been so busy telling everyone Art was guilty, when I decided I had to get rid of him, I figured I'd let you be the main one accusing him. I knew you'd think it was him driving. I hid some drugs in his apartment, too. I thought that would help, but he found them."

That must have been what he'd been talking about when he'd threatened her in the darkroom, Jessie thought. Not the lens cap. He must have searched after she'd broken in and found the steroids and realized Val was framing him. He should have realized it meant Val was planning to kill him. They passed a pull-off on the left, under the cliff, and she slowed. The turnoff to the picnic grounds was just ahead.

Val had fallen silent. Now she said, "All right, pull off." They were at the turnoff.

Jessie stopped the car. She reached for the key, but Val told her, "No, leave it running. Now back around so we're facing the road again." Jessie followed directions, leaving the car pointed toward the pavement and a narrow cut between the cliffs. "Just put it in park." Jessie did so, her pulse hammering so hard, she could hear it. She saw what Val had in mind. The most dangerous part of Gates Pass, the section where dozens of wrecks had occurred over the years, was through the tight cut thirty feet away. The road curved sharply to the left, going down the side of the mountain above an almost-sheer five-hundred-foot drop. Val must be planning to use the knife, then send the car over the cliff. She'd probably roll around some in the dirt, mess herself up. Randy was convinced Art was the killer. All Val would have to do was claim Art had had his knife. It would be easy to make up a story. If both Jessie and Art were dead, Randy would back Val up. Art would take the blame, and Val would be regarded as a victim who got away, the sole survivor. Randy might even turn to her for comfort, Jessie thought bitterly, and no doubt Val would be happy to claim him, now that Art had proved to be a mistake.

"Unfasten your seat belt," Val directed. Of course, she wanted to make sure they had no chance of survival. Jessie did so, her fingers fumbling on the release. Her hands were numb with fear. "Now, hold still. . . ." Val increased the pressure on the knife while she reached behind her, trying to unfasten Art's belt. Carefully, Jessie felt beside her with her left hand for the door handle. If she could open the door . . .

There was a click as Val managed to get Art's seat belt unfastened. He moaned and stirred again, and Jessie's heart started pounding more wildly than ever. "Art, wake up!" she said urgently, then cried out in pain as the knife dug in viciously. Beyond Val, Art mumbled, then said, "Val?"

"It doesn't matter," Val said, ignoring Art. "Jessie, I'm sorry, but this is my only chance. I'm sorry."

For a moment the knife was pulled back, then Jessie screamed as a line of fire cut across her side. She tugged at the door handle and it came open. Val stabbed at her again as she fell out the door, catching her on the hip this time. She dived after Jessie, stabbing down as Jessie rolled away from the car, scrambling up to her knees as Val pulled herself across the driver's seat and half fell out of the car. Behind her, Art roused himself again and called out, "Jessie!"

"Get out of the car, Art!" Jessie screamed as she tried to get the rest of the way to her feet. Her side felt as if it had been branded where the knife had ripped its way along it. A rib had turned the blade. Jessie half crawled, half scrambled for the rear of the car. Her right hip was on fire, too, and she wasn't sure it would bear her weight. Val held the knife to one side, panting, as she came after her.

"It won't do any good, Jessie," she said, then flung herself at Jessie, knife stabbing out. Jessie rolled under the trunk of the car, burning her arm on the exhaust pipe. She barely noticed, though, as Val dropped to her knees and tried to reach under the car. Jessie wriggled forward on her belly, farther under the car. The weight of the vehicle shifted above her, as the passenger's door swung open and Art got out. He hauled himself up on the side of the car, and Val cursed and stood up.

As soon as she did, Jessie rolled out on the opposite side, across from Art. "Give up, Val," she panted. "You can't get us both." That wasn't true—Art was still half unconscious, and she was losing blood. She didn't know how bad her side was, but the pain had her gasping. Jessie forced herself to stand up. She was dizzy, but she'd have a fighting chance if she was on her feet. Across from her, Art was hanging on to the passenger's door, swaying on his feet as he shifted the weight off his bad leg. Jessie leaned against the side of the car. The metal vibrated under her hands, the engine still running.

Val stood at the rear of the car, looking from Art back to Jessie, the bloody knife gripped tightly. The Mustang's lights were still on, and with both doors open, the interior light was on as well, illuminating them all like something out of a nightmare, and throwing bizarre shadows on the cliffs around them. Holding on to the side of the car, Art took a step toward the rear of the Mustang, then stopped.

"Val." It looked as though he was trying to work himself up into the rage that let him play football without heeding injuries, but he was too close to passing out, and his leg wouldn't support him anymore.

Val took a step back, holding the knife higher in front of her. "Stay back, Art. Just stay away from me." She took another step. The breath sobbed in Jessie's throat as she wondered if she should throw herself into the driver's seat and try to get away. She couldn't. Art had known the truth, but he hadn't been the killer, and if Jessie left, they'd be at each other's throats long before she could get help.

Art reached the rear of the convertible and stood there swaying, using the trunk of the car to support himself. Val took a couple of steps sideways toward the road, her eyes never leaving him. There was a flash as headlights appeared around the farthest curve, coming faster than was safe on the icy road. Then everything happened at once.

With a yell Art tried to launch a tackle at Val, pushing himself off the car. He stumbled as he reached her but still pulled her down just as a car slid to a halt behind them, stopping on the road. Jessie let out a cry and ran toward the couple on the ground as Val screamed and brought down the knife. There was a groan, and Art rolled away.

"Jessie!" Randy ran toward them, his feet slipping on the ice as he reached Art and bent over him. He grabbed Art and hauled him up, his heavy left fist drawing back for a blow when Jessie reached him and grabbed his arm.

"It wasn't Art!" Jessie screamed. Val ran for the driver's door of the Mustang and fell into the seat. Randy paused, suddenly seeing the blood that was already soaking Art's side, as the door slammed. "Stop her!" Jessie grabbed Art, and Randy released him, sprinting for the car. Art's deadweight nearly threw Jessie off her feet. Jessie eased him to the ground, almost dropping him, and went after Randy. But before Randy could take a second step, the Mustang's tires spun, then took hold as the car jumped forward. Val accelerated. Randy stopped as Jessie ran to join him.

The passenger's door was open, swinging wildly. There was a clang as it hit the side of the narrow pass, and the rear of the car fishtailed around the curve, still accelerating. Jessie and Randy ran frantically toward the cut, his strong arms supporting her. They reached the top just as the back end of the car skidded off the pavement. A single high-pitched scream echoed above the crash of metal as the Mustang left the road, hit the side of the mountain, and rolled, end over end, to the bottom of the cliff. The echoes seemed to last for a long time.

Randy and Jessie stood at the top of the cliff, staring down. For several long moments after the reverberations ended, they stood there, not speaking. One headlight had somehow survived the crash, beaming back up the cliff, painting a white ghost of light on the side of the mountain. There was another faint crash as the wreck settled further.

"Do you think she's . . ." Jessie stopped. She was shaking, and all of a sudden her side was throbbing with renewed pain.

"She's dead," Randy said grimly. He held her closer and felt the stickiness of blood. "Jessie! Are you all right?"

"I don't know," she admitted. Her knees started to give way, and he caught her round the waist again as they started back toward his Toyota. "Val had a knife."

"Not Art?" They had reached Art's ominously still form, where Jessie had dropped him. Gingerly she let herself down onto her knees beside him and carefully rolled him over.

She let out a sigh of relief as his eyes flickered open for an instant, then rolled back in his head as he passed out again.

"He's alive," she said thankfully. "She didn't kill him."

"Jessie, what's been going on?" Randy sounded confused, and she didn't blame him. She'd been confused for weeks, looking at things from the wrong perspective.

"It was Val all along," she said. "And she was trying to kill me and Art, and make it look as though he'd murdered me and had been killed getting away. And it almost worked—except in the end, Val was the one who died."

She stood up. "It's a long story. I'll tell you on the way back into town."

"I'd better get both of you to a hospital," he said. "Only I don't know if we should move Art."

"M'okay." Art's eyes were open again, despite the blood soaking his side. His ribs hadn't stopped the blade, but he was still alive. "Get me outta here."

Moving slowly and carefully, the two of them got Art into the front seat of Randy's car. Jessie climbed in after him, almost passing out as the loss of blood began to catch up with her. Randy, his right hand so swollen he could barely handle the wheel, backed the car around, then headed slowly down the mountain toward the distant lights of Tucson, and a hospital, and Detective Gutierrez.

Behind them, one headlight still shone from the pile of wreckage at the bottom of Gates Pass.

Don't miss
Deadly Stranger
by M. C. Sumner

One

Kelly Tallon came awake at the first note of music from the clock radio. She smiled to herself. Her parents had been convinced that she wouldn't get up this early on the first day of spring break. But her parents had never understood Kelly's obsession with skiing. For a week of spring skiing in Colorado, she would have gotten up at four in the morning every day for a year.

Fumbling in the dark, she found the switch and managed to shut off the alarm. Across the room, her younger sister Amanda muttered something in her sleep, and the springs of her bed squeaked as she rolled over.

Kelly climbed out of bed. The hardwood floor was cool under her bare feet. She navigated through the darkness until her hands found the clothes she had left across a chair. She peeled her nightshirt over her head and tossed it back toward the bed, slid into her jeans, and pulled on a cotton sweatshirt.

She stepped carefully across the room toward the dresser. Her searching fingers picked out a brush in the pile of objects that covered the dresser's top. Squinting at the mirror above the dresser, Kelly ran the brush through her chin-length auburn hair. She wished she could turn on the lights.

One more summer, she thought. *I just have to get through this summer and I'll be out on my own.* College was only months away, and Kelly was anxious to get out of her house, out of her high school—on with her life. She smiled, and she could just see the reflection of her white teeth in the darkened mirror.

She found her soft-sided suitcase where she'd left it by the door and hefted it with her left hand. The bag was heavy, filled with a week's worth of clothes. Kelly leaned far to the right as she opened the door, and staggered out into the hallway.

Her skis and ski poles were waiting at the top of the stairs. The skis were several inches longer than Kelly was tall. Getting them balanced across her right shoulder was quite a trick. The combination of heavy bag and lengthy skis made her wobble as she walked down the hallway, the tips of her skis drawing figure-eights in the air.

She turned to go down the stairs, and the skis cracked loudly against the wall. Kelly cringed. She stopped, waiting to see if there was any reaction.

When no one stirred, she started down again. Two steps later, the skis hit the wall a second time. After that, Kelly took the steps very, very slowly.

She had to put her bag down to get the front door open. Stepping out into the cool morning air, she pulled her bag through, and carefully eased the door shut behind her. Stars still shone overhead, but the sky in the east was turning gray-pink. A quarter moon floated between wispy clouds and reflected silver light from a yard covered in dew. Kelly walked across the grass, leaving dark footprints behind her. She sat her suitcase down by the curb and waited.

She didn't have to wait long. There was a screech of tires from the corner, and headlights spilled down the empty street. A blue Mustang, looking black in the moonlight, came sliding around the corner, sped down the street, and stopped in front of Kelly's house with a final squeal of burning rubber. Lauren Miki threw her door open and stepped out onto the road.

"Morning," Kelly said cheerfully.

"It's not morning—the sun's not even up," Lauren replied. She arched her back and stretched. "Come on, Kel. Let's get your skis loaded."

Kelly had taken two steps toward Lauren, before her mouth dropped open in surprise. "Lauren! What happened to your hair?"

Lauren reached a hand up to the nape of her neck and ran a finger across the bare skin. Her black hair was cut short in the back and sides, with thick bangs left to tumble across her forehead. "What do you think?" she asked.

Kelly tilted her head to one side and studied her friend for a moment. "It suits you," she said at last. "It really shows off your face. But it's a bit of a shock; you've had long hair since the second grade."

"Yeah, well, it's time to make some changes."

Lauren stepped onto the grass and took the skis from Kelly. Almost a foot taller than Kelly, Lauren handled the skis with ease. She slid them under an arrangement of cords and straps that crisscrossed the Mustang's roof.

"Are you sure that rack you rigged up is going to work?" Kelly asked skeptically.

"Absolutely. I've got my skis in it, too."

"All right. Just as long as my skis don't end up on the interstate somewhere in Kansas."

Lauren popped the hatch open and tossed in Kelly's bag. Packed together with Lauren's luggage, it made for a tight fit, and it took Lauren two tries to get the cover closed. As it finally clicked shut, a light came on in the upper floor of Kelly's house.

"Let's get going," Lauren said softly.

Kelly opened her door and started to get in, but another light came on in the house. She climbed back out of the car.

Lauren was fumbling for her keys. "Where are you going?" she asked, and Kelly was surprised at the tension in her voice.

196

"It's probably just my Dad. I'm sure he just . . ."

"Get in," Lauren hissed.

"But . . ."

"Get in!"

She said it with such authority that Kelly didn't even think about arguing. She dropped into her seat and slammed the door. A moment later, Lauren found the right key and ground the Mustang's motor to life. They shot off down the street just as the outside light of Kelly's house snapped on.

Looking back, Kelly could see a figure coming out her front door. "What was that all about?"

"What was what all about?" Lauren asked. She had a habit of evading questions by repeating them—a habit that always drove Kelly nuts.

"Why were you in such a hurry to leave?" Kelly said. "I'm sure my dad just wanted to give me his 'Be careful' speech."

"Maybe," Lauren said. She shifted the Mustang through its gears and made the turn at the corner so fast that Kelly was thrown up against her door. The back tires lost their grip on the blacktop, and the car began to spin wildly. Then Lauren fought it under control.

"God, Lauren," Kelly said, her fingers tightly gripping her seat. "Are you trying to get us killed? What's going on?"

"I didn't want you to talk to your dad, because your dad probably got a call from my dad," Lauren said. A traffic light turned red ahead of them, and Kelly was

197

grateful that Lauren brought the car to a stop.

"So what was your dad going to say?"

Lauren looked over at her. Even in the dim light, her dark brown eyes were bright with emotion. "He probably told your dad I don't have permission to go on this trip."

For the second time that morning, Kelly felt her mouth drop open. "Lauren! Why would he say that? I was there when he gave you permission. We've been planning this for months."

A car honked behind them, and they both looked up to see that the light had turned green. Lauren accelerated away from the intersection. "It's my grades," she said.

"You've got great grades. When's the last time you made below a B?"

"Not my regular grades, my grades on the SATs."

Kelly frowned. "But I thought you did fine on those."

"Fine is not fine enough, my dear," Lauren replied, putting on a snooty accent. "Not if one expects to attend college within the selective ranks of the Ivy League."

"Now I'm really confused. I thought you were going to Southwest State?"

"Yeah, that's where I want to go. But of course, where I want to go doesn't count for anything." Lauren steered the car across the highway onto the access ramp for the interstate. Even this early on a Saturday, the interstate was half-choked with trucks and cars. Behind them, sun peeked over the horizon, and orange light shone across the highway, flashing from glass and chrome.

Kelly watched Lauren as she moved the car from lane to lane. She had always envied Lauren's beauty and maturity. Her height and figure had let Lauren pass for a college student before she was old enough to drive. Kelly hadn't grown an inch since she was twelve, and even at eighteen, people still mistook her for an eighth-grader.

Where Lauren had never had any shortage of boyfriends, Kelly's dates had been few and far between. While Kelly went through high school almost unnoticed, Lauren had been on several sports teams, a class officer almost every year, and a leader in more clubs than Kelly could count.

And then there was the money. Kelly's family wasn't exactly poor; they had a nice house and all the standard stuff. But Lauren's family had a huge house, and Lauren always had a new car and fancy clothes. Lauren was rich.

It was easy to be jealous of Lauren, but there was one thing that Kelly had never envied: Lauren's father. In all the times she'd met Mr. Miki, Kelly didn't think she'd ever seen him smile. No matter what Lauren did, it never seemed good enough for him. When Lauren got an A, he wanted it to be an A plus. When Lauren made cheerleader, he wanted her to be head cheerleader. When Lauren was on the volleyball team, he wanted her to be the star of the team.

"What are we going to do now?" Kelly asked.

"What do you mean?"

"Well, we can't go all the way to Colorado without permission."

"Why not," Lauren said. There was a tone in her voice that made Kelly nervous.

"For one thing, we'll get killed when we get home."

Lauren gave a choked laugh. "My dad's already as mad as he's going to get."

"Yeah, but my dad's not that mad yet," Kelly said.

"Don't tell him."

Kelly frowned. "Don't tell him what?"

"Don't tell him you knew I wasn't supposed to go." Lauren paused to slide the car across two lanes and slammed on the gas to get around a line of slower moving traffic. "He can't get mad at you if you didn't know you were doing anything wrong."

Kelly thought about it for a moment, then shook her head. "Won't work. As soon as we get there, I'm supposed to call in. And as soon as I do, my dad will tell me to beat it back home."

"What if you don't call?" Lauren suggested.

"If I don't call, he'll probably have the National Guard after us. It's the one thing he made me promise to do every day."

"We could tell him the phone wasn't working."

"That might work for the first night," Kelly said. "But then what?"

Lauren slapped her hands against the steering wheel. "I don't know!" She closed her eyes for a second, and Kelly fought the temptation to grab the wheel. But the car stayed straight until Lauren opened her eyes. "I don't know," she repeated more softly, "but I'll figure out something by the time we get there."

Kelly put a hand on her friend's arm. "I think this is a bad idea, Lauren. You know how much I wanted to go on this trip, but I think the best thing we can do is go home. Maybe if we talk to your dad, he'll change his mind."

"He won't change his mind," Lauren insisted. Her dark eyes were fixed on the road ahead. "I'm going."

"Lauren . . ."

"No. If you want me to take you back home, I will. But I'm going."

Kelly bit her lip and tried to figure out the right thing to do. If she went home, she wouldn't be in trouble, but there was no telling what Lauren would do. In the mood she was in, Kelly didn't doubt that she might go on the trip by herself. And she wasn't sure that Lauren would come back.

"All right," Kelly said at last. "I'll go. I still think it's the wrong thing, but I'll go."

"Thanks, Kel. We'll have fun, just wait and see."

"Yeah, well, I hope so. But I still don't see how we're going to keep from being shipped straight home as soon as we get there."

A smile came to Lauren's lips. "I can think of some pretty twisted ways to get there. If we don't have to check in with your dad until we get to Colorado, we might have longer than you think."

"Just as long as you don't try to drive to Colorado by way of California," Kelly said. "That might be kind of hard to explain."

"We could still go to Florida, like I wanted to do in the first place." Lauren's face brightened, and she seemed to shake off her anger. "Anyway, at least we'll have the trip. I love to drive."

"I'm glad you do, because I sure don't." Kelly looked out the window at the shopping strips and gas stations that clustered around each exit of the highway. "How long is this going to take—assuming no detours through L.A.?"

"St. Louis to Denver is about twenty hours each way, I guess," Lauren said. "And we better figure on another couple of hours to get to the resort. If we drive hard, we should make it there sometime tomorrow."

Kelly sighed. Twenty something hours each way, plus whatever time they took to eat or sleep. It was a long way to go just to get yelled at. "Promise me one thing, okay?"

"What's that?"

"Promise me that no matter what else happens, I get to make at least one run down the slopes."

Lauren raised her right hand like someone being sworn in for court. "I solemnly swear that Kelly Tallon will not end this spring break without getting a chance to ski."

"Good," Kelly said. "Now, no matter what happens, it'll be worth it."

Two

Kelly jerked awake from a dream of falling. A radio was playing loudly, and she fumbled to her right, trying to find the switch to shut off the alarm. Her hand hit smooth glass. She blinked and pushed her hair back from her eyes. Then she remembered that she was in Lauren's car on the way to Colorado.

"You okay?" Lauren asked.

"Yeah, I've just never been very good at sleeping in cars."

Kelly sat up and looked through her window. They were passing fields where the brilliant green of spring wheat was just starting to poke through the brown earth. The sky overhead was a very dark gray, and looked even darker ahead.

"Where are we?" she asked.

Lauren pulled a map from the space between the seats and passed it to Kelly. "I think we're about thirty miles from Kansas City. There's an exit coming up. See if you can find it on the map."

Kelly read the green sign on the road and ran her finger down the line of the interstate on the map until she found the small town she was looking for. "I don't think we've gone as far as you think. It looks more like fifty or sixty miles."

"One lane of the highway was closed back there," Lauren said. "We went about thirty miles an hour while you were asleep."

The dark sky caught Kelly's attention. Among the knots of gray cloud, there were streaks of greenish yellow that looked like bruises in the air. "Radio say anything about a storm?"

"Uh-uh."

"Looks like a big one up there. I'm surprised they haven't been saying anything."

"Nope," Lauren said. "But I've been listening to music stations."

Seconds later, scattered drops of rain began to smash against the Mustang's windshield. Kelly leaned her face against the side window and looked up at the sky. The blackened clouds were heaving up and down. "Wow," she said. "It really looks bad."

Over the next few minutes, the rain grew harder and the wind stronger. The sky got so dark that it was hard to believe that the sun hadn't set. Lauren barely slowed, even when they began to pass other cars that had pulled over to wait out the storm.

"You sure you can see okay?" Kelly asked.

"I can see," Lauren said. "As long as it doesn't get any worse." She had barely finished speaking when there was a sudden bang from the hood of the car. "What was that?"

There was another bang, and a sharp crack as something struck the windshield. Kelly saw a white lump glance off the fender of the car, and another bounce along the dark shoulder of the road.

"It's hail!" she shouted. "Big hail."

"It's going to beat my car to death," Lauren cried. There was another bang of hail against the roof, and another against the hood.

Kelly squinted through the gray sheets of wind-driven rain and hail. "It looks like there's a bridge over the road up ahead. If we can get under that . . ."

"You got it!" Lauren leaned far forward as she steered along a road that neither of them could clearly see. The sound of impacting hail increased until Kelly felt like she was inside a popcorn machine. The racket was deafening.

Kelly thought it was a good thing that all the other traffic had pulled off, because she didn't know how Lauren could possibly spot any other cars in time to keep from hitting them. Then the shadow of the bridge became visible just ahead. The second they slipped under it, the deafening sound of the hail cut off like someone had thrown a switch.

Lauren steered the car to the side of the road. For a second, the girls just sat there, catching their breath. Kelly was breathing so hard, she felt as if she had pushed the car those last hundred yards down the highway.

"Look at the hood," Lauren said.

Kelly looked, and saw dozens of small circular dents in the sheet metal of the car's hood. She opened her door and stepped out, and Lauren did the same. "It's not too bad," Kelly said.

"Not bad? Look at my car! It's got more dents than a waffle!"

"When the sun comes out, it'll probably pop out most of them."

Lightning struck somewhere close by, and thunder boomed under the bridge like a bomb blast. Lauren and Kelly jumped. Kelly saw Lauren's eyes round and white against her tan skin. Lauren stared back for a moment, and then she surprised Kelly by bursting into laughter.

"What is wrong with you?" Kelly asked.

Lauren waved her hand and fought to hold down her laughter. "It's just . . . it's just that you looked so funny! With your eyes popping out and everything."

Kelly shook her head. "You are nuts, girl."

"I know," Lauren said. She managed to strangle the last bit of her laughter, just as another clap of thunder shook the ground under their feet. Somewhere in the distance, a high-pitched siren began to blow. "What's that? Fire engine? Something started by the lightning?"

"I don't think so," Kelly said after a moment. "I think it's a tornado warning."

Lauren tilted her head back and looked upward.

"Great. What is this, some kind of sign? Well it's not going to work. I'm going on this trip, and that's that." Lightning flashed close by and they both jumped again.

"At least I don't see any tornado coming," Kelly said. They leaned against the car and watched as the hail pounded on the roadway away from the bridge. Every now and then, a gust of wind brought some of the rain almost to their feet, and the girls flinched every time the thunder crashed. A single car went zipping past them so quickly that they barely saw it before it had vanished behind the wall of rain and hail.

"There's somebody in a hurry," Kelly said.

"And somebody that doesn't care about their car," Lauren added.

A few minutes later, the lightning began to lessen and the distant wail of the siren went away. The hail vanished, and the rain settled down to a steady drizzle. Most of the storm seemed to have passed to the east, leaving a gray overcast sky in the west that promised days of rain.

"Think we should go now?" Kelly asked.

"I guess so." Lauren opened the driver's door and started to get in.

"Lauren," Kelly said softly.

Lauren leaned back out. "What?"

"Maybe we should go home. I mean, this isn't exactly the best start to the trip. And with your dad and everything. Maybe it *is* some kind of sign."

Lauren ran a hand through her short hair. Kelly

207

could see that the resolve she had shown that morning had been eroded by the storm. But finally, she shook her head. "No, let's go on."

"Do you really think we should?" Kelly asked.

"Of course I do. Just wait," Lauren replied. "Good things are going to start to happen soon."

The storm had filled the ditches at the side of the road with rivers of surging water and turned the green fields into dark brown mud. Kelly saw some trees down beside a distant white house and a truck mired in the water-choked ruts of a dirt road.

They had gone only a few miles when they passed a green sedan on the side of the road. It was an old car, and its squared-off sides showed the dents of the hailstorm. The hood was up, and as they went past, a figure waved at them from the driver's window.

Lauren slowed and turned her head to look back at the car. "Is that the car that passed us while we were waiting?"

Kelly thought for a moment. "I'm not sure. It could be."

Lauren pulled over to the side of the road, stopped, and shifted the Mustang into reverse. "Let's see what his trouble is."

"Why don't we just go on to the next exit and tell somebody to come back for him?" Kelly asked. "It might not be such a great idea to stop out here in the middle of nowhere."

"Come on, Kel. If we want good things to happen, we have to do good things, right?"

"Sounds right," Kelly agreed. "But let's do good things someplace else, okay?"

Lauren kept backing up. The green sedan appeared through the haze of the drizzle, and the driver got out and started jogging toward the Mustang. Lauren rolled down the window as he approached.

"Thanks for stopping," the guy said. "I was afraid I would be stuck here for hours."

From the passenger seat, Kelly couldn't see the man very well—a strong chin, slightly curly dark hair, a flash of white teeth between smiling lips—that was all. But she didn't have to see him to know what he looked like; Lauren's response told her everything.

Lauren tilted her head slightly and put on a knowing smile. "I'm just glad we could help," she said. Her voice was half an octave lower than normal and it oozed sophistication. "Would you like us to send someone back for you?" She paused for a moment, and her smile widened. "Or would you like a ride to the next gas station?"

"I wouldn't want to cause you any trouble . . ."

"It's no problem," Lauren said. "Climb in."

"Thanks," the man said. "Let me go lock up the car and get a couple of things, and I'll be right back." He trotted back down the rainy highway.

"I still think this is a bad idea," Kelly said.

Lauren turned to her and raised an eyebrow. "Did you get a good look at him?"

"Not really."

"Just wait till you do."

209

"Look," Kelly said. "I'm sure he's cute, but shouldn't we just send someone for him? I mean, it's not safe to pick people up off the side of the road."

"Relax, it's only until the next exit."

Kelly started to make one last protest, but she was interrupted by a rapping against her window. She turned to see the guy looking in at her.

At first she thought Lauren was wrong—there was nothing special about him. He was average. He was young, maybe no older than they were, maybe college age. His faded denim jacket fit loosely over a trim build. *Okay*, she thought, *he is pretty good looking, but nothing to get all that worked up about*. Then Kelly saw his eyes. His eyes were blue. Not blue like most blue eyes, but an incredibly deep blue like sapphires. Those eyes transformed his face.

Without thinking about it, Kelly pushed her door open and climbed out into the drizzle. She felt nervous, as if the guy was going to ask her out instead of bumming a ride in Lauren's car. "Uh, the back seat's pretty cramped," she said. "Maybe I better ride back there."

"No," he said. "It's enough that you're giving me a ride. I'm not going to kick you out of your seat. I'll be fine in the back."

Kelly stood aside as he pulled her seat forward and slid into the small rear seat of the Mustang. "You're sure you fit back there?" she asked as she climbed back into the front.

"I'm fine," he said. Kelly got another flash of his

very white teeth as he gave her a quick smile, then he turned toward Lauren. "I really appreciate you ladies rescuing me like this."

"We're happy to help," Lauren said. "You have everything you need out of your car?"

He held up a small leather satchel in his right hand. "Right here."

"Then let's get going." Lauren hit the gas and shifted the gears as the Mustang sped up. The rain had dropped off enough to crank the wipers down to a very slow speed. In the distance, a dull-orange glow at the base of the clouds showed that the sun had almost set.

"My name's Marshall," the man said as they left the green sedan behind. Kelly thought there was something unusual in his voice. Maybe it was a trace of a southern accent, maybe it was just his relaxed, slow way of talking. Whatever it was, it made her feel comfortable.

Lauren spoke up. "Hi, Marshall, I'm Lauren." She took one hand off the wheel and stretched her arm toward the backseat to exchange a quick shake.

Kelly turned in her seat. "Kelly." She reached out her hand, and Marshall took it. He held it for a long moment between fingers that were strong and had the slight roughness that came from hard work.

"You girls on vacation?" he asked.

"How'd you guess?" Lauren asked.

"Spring break?"

"Yeah," Lauren said. "You, too?"

"You got it. Let me guess, you two are . . . juniors?"

211

"Seniors," Lauren told him.

"Wow, seniors. What college?"

"Oh, we're still in high school," Kelly said.

Lauren glanced over at her with a look that could have cut glass, and Kelly realized that she had just stomped on the image Lauren had been constructing. "But only for one more month," she finished weakly.

"I never would have guessed you were still in high school," Marshall said. "You look older."

Kelly could feel the blood rise in her face and hoped her blush wasn't obvious in the dim light. She knew he was talking only about Lauren. No one, but no one, had ever thought Kelly looked older than she was. Younger, all the time, but never older.

"What about you?" Lauren asked. "Are you in college?"

"I just finished up a pre-med course," Marshall said. "I guess I'll start med school in the fall, but I'm still trying to decide where."

Kelly was surprised. She wouldn't have thought Marshall was old enough to be out of college already, and his clothes, car, and rough hands didn't match her idea of a medical student. But maybe he had gotten through school on a scholarship. And if he was as young as he looked, maybe he had been one of those genius kids that started college years early. Or maybe, like Kelly, he just looked younger than he was.

"Have you made college plans yet, Lauren?" Marshall asked.

"Well, if it were up to me, I'd be heading for the

West Coast. But my dad wants me back east some-where."

"Well, if you'll excuse me for giving advice, I don't think you should listen to your dad. The West Coast is a great place to be in college."

"My dad thinks that the Ivy League schools are the only place to get a good education," Lauren said.

"Maybe fifty years ago," Marshall said, "but not today. Go where you want to go. You're only in college once. Why spend four years in a place you don't want to be?"

"I wish my dad could hear you say that! He won't listen to me, but a med student that's been to those schools . . . Maybe he'd listen to you."

"Hey, if you think it would help, I'll be happy to give him a call."

Lauren began to talk about her father and all the things he'd put her through. For the most part, Marshall listened quietly, interjecting a comment every now and then, or asking a few questions. He gave the impression that he was hanging on her every word.

Kelly felt left out. She looked for a chance to get back in the conversation, but Lauren was on a roll, and Kelly couldn't get a word in edgewise. She leaned her head against the cool glass of the window and watched the darkening countryside roll past.

A few minutes later, the car rolled over a gentle rise. A mile up the road was an exit ramp, and just a few hundred yards from the intersection was a sprawling truck stop.

"Look," Kelly said. "There's a place we can see about getting a tow."

Lauren stopped her story about her father in mid-sentence and turned to look at the approaching truck stop. "I don't know. That place doesn't look like they'd notice anything that had less than a dozen wheels. They might not even have a tow truck."

"We'd better check," Kelly said. "We're probably twenty miles from Marshall's car already. If we go any farther, it'll cost him a fortune to tow it."

"Kelly's right," Marshall said. "We'd probably better stop."

Lauren pursed her lips, but she nodded and guided the car onto the exit ramp. There were a dozen semi-trucks clustered around the pumps and washing bays of the truck stop. They made metal walls that Lauren had to steer between to find the front. At the entrance, they could see a small restaurant.

"Why don't we get something to eat first?" Lauren suggested. "We haven't stopped in hours."

Kelly wished she could say that she didn't want to eat at this place. The white brick walls of the building had been splashed with mud from the passing trucks, and the inside didn't look much cleaner. But she realized that what Lauren wanted was not a chance to eat, but an excuse to spend a few more minutes with Marshall. "Okay," she said. "Sounds good."

They climbed out of the car, and Kelly stretched, trying to work the stiffness of the long ride out of her arms and legs. The door opened, and one of the men inside the restaurant came out. He was a pot-bellied man with arms as big as hams and dark hair that was streaked with gray. He had his arm tight around the waist of a pretty girl that looked to be high school age or younger.

"Are you sure you're going all the way to L.A.?" the girl asked.

"Sure, honey," said the tall man. "Don't you want to get to California?"

"I guess," the girl said. She followed the man to one of the parked trucks and he boosted her up into the cab. Kelly couldn't hear the rest of their conversation, but she could hear the man laughing as he climbed in. She thought the girl was pretty stupid—or pretty desperate—to get in that truck, and she wondered if the girl would ever see L.A.

"Let's get inside," Lauren said.

Kelly nodded and followed Marshall and Lauren into the small restaurant. There was a sign over the largest part of the room that said "Truck Drivers Only." What was left was a pair of booths crammed into the space beside the kitchen door.

"I think we better sit over there," Marshall said. "No one is going to mistake you two for truck drivers."

Kelly thought about the girl in the parking lot. No one would have taken her for a truck driver either.

Marshall waited while the two girls slipped into a booth, then took a seat next to Lauren. "Cheer up," he said to Kelly. "The food in these places is usually pretty good."

Kelly took a plastic menu from the rack at the back of the table and looked over the options. It was the expected collection of sandwiches and dinner plates.

The waitress, a middle-aged woman in a faded blue uniform dress, came over to the table. "You ready to order?" she asked.

"Burger and fries," Lauren said without looking at the menu.

"Sounds good," Marshall said. "I'll have the same."

Kelly scanned the menu, trying to find something that wasn't drenched in grease. "Can I just get a green salad?"

"Sure," the waitress said. She scribbled their order on her pad. "Be up in just a minute."

As she walked away, Marshall stood. "While we're waiting for our food, I think I'll go check on getting my car towed. Okay?"

"Okay," Lauren said. "Want me to come with you?"

"You better wait," he said. "I'll be right back." He went to the front of the restaurant and shoved the glass door open. He waited a moment, holding the door while a man in a green T-shirt came in and walked into the truck drivers' section of the little restaurant. As he slipped out the door, Marshall turned to flash one last smile.

"What do you think?" Lauren said as soon as the door had closed.

"About what?" Kelly asked.

"You know. About Marshall."

Kelly picked up a saltshaker shaped like a tiny

truck and turned it around in her hand. "I don't know. He's cute."

"He's more than cute," Lauren said. "Way more. And he's a med student."

"Yeah, he's really nice, but what does it matter? We're going to Colorado, and he's going . . . wherever it is he's going."

Lauren frowned for a moment. "You know, I don't think we ever talked about that. I wonder where he is going?"

"Good evenin'," said a voice.

Kelly looked up and saw the trucker in the green shirt standing above them. He was well over six feet tall, and his shoulders were thick with muscle. A baseball cap was pulled low over his dark blond hair, but not low enough to hide the edge of a bald spot. His gray eyes were fixed on Lauren. "You need a ride tonight, little lady?" he asked.

Lauren looked up at him in confusion. "Ride?"

"We don't need a ride," Kelly said. "Thanks anyway."

The trucker's eyes shifted over to Kelly, and scanned her as if he were seeing her for the first time. "I wasn't asking you, kid." He turned back to Lauren. "Come on, sugar. Let's go for a ride in a big rig." He reached down a large hand to Lauren.

She leaned away from him. "I've . . . I've got a car," she sputtered.

"A car's only a car," he said. His beefy fingers closed on her, shoulder and he let his hand drift

217

across the soft material of her sweater.

Kelly reached across the table and grabbed his arm. "We're just waiting for a friend."

The trucker didn't bother to look at her this time. "Don't worry, I can be friendly."

Lauren looked over at Kelly. Her dark eyes, usually so confident, seemed lost.

Kelly looked around for the waitress, for some other customers, for anybody. But the room was empty. She started to push herself up from her seat. She wasn't sure what she could do against this guy, but she had to do something.

The glass door of the restaurant swung open and Marshall came striding in. He stopped one step inside the door, and his deep-blue eyes locked on the trucker. "What's the problem here?" he said.

The trucker looked up. "There's no problem here, sonny. I was just taking this lady for a ride."

Marshall took two slow steps closer to the table. "Maybe the lady doesn't want a ride."

"Butt out," the trucker said, but he took his hand off Lauren and straightened up to face Marshall. "This is none of your business."

Marshall took another step. He was no more than three feet from the trucker. Kelly could see the muscles in the trucker's arms knotting as he clinched his hands into fists. "Lauren," Marshall said softly. "Did this man hurt you?"

"No," Lauren said.

"Not yet," Kelly added.

"Then everything's okay." Marshall nodded his head toward the empty trucker's side of the restaurant. "If you could just go back to your seat, we can go on with our dinner."

"Sure," the trucker said. "As soon as the lady tells me herself. I'm going to . . ." started the trucker.

Marshall's hand pistoned out as fast as a striking snake and hit the bigger man in the chest. The trucker's gray eyes bugged out and he staggered backward. A honking noise came from his mouth as he fought to pull in a breath.

Marshall turned to Kelly. "Why don't you take Lauren out to the car," he said. His voice was still so very calm, completely unhurried, but there was something in his eyes—a light that hadn't been there before. "I'll find the waitress and see if I can get our food to go."

The trucker managed to pull in a long whistling breath. He coughed. "You son of a . . ."

Marshall hit him again. This time the big man didn't just stagger, he fell like a puppet with its strings cut.

"Is he okay?" Kelly asked.

"He'll be fine in a few minutes," Marshall said. "I just hit him in the solar maxus. Come on, there's no tow truck here. Let's just forget the waitress and get something at another place." He held out a hand to Lauren, and she took it quickly.

She climbed to her feet and followed him toward the door. They were almost out before she turned back

219

to Kelly. "You coming, Kel?" she asked.

"Sure. I'll be right there." Kelly watched them go out the door, then took a look at the man on the floor. When he groaned and turned over on his side, she was relieved.

At the front door, she paused and watched Marshall guiding Lauren across the wet parking lot. Kelly might have had only a couple of high school biology classes, but she knew that the place where Marshall had punched the guy was called the solar plexus, not the solar maxus.

Would a guy that had graduated pre-med make a mistake like that? Kelly didn't know. She pushed open the door and walked out.

Three

"Sorry to keep you running around like this," Marshall said.

"Are you kidding?" Lauren said. "After the way you took care of that jerk at the truck stop, you deserve a medal or something."

"It's really unfortunate that this had to happen. You know, most truckers are really decent guys. Don't let this give you a bad impression of them."

"You think this next place will have a towing service?" Kelly asked.

"That's what they said at the last place," Marshall replied.

Since leaving the truck stop, they had been to three other places along the interstate. One even had a tow truck parked in front, but Marshall had come back out saying that the truck was broken. By now, they were getting close to Kansas City, and Marshall's old green sedan was thirty or forty miles back down the road. Kelly was beginning to wonder if they would ever find a place to go back for it.

"Where are you going, anyway, Marshall?" Kelly asked.

"Just on my way to visit some friends out west," he replied.

Kelly waited for him to go on, but that seemed to be all he was going to say. "Sounds nice. Where at?"

"Oh, some different places," he said. "Hey, there's our exit."

At this exit the road was lined with fast-food places and a couple of cheap motels. There were two gas stations, but neither of them had a garage or any sign of a towing service.

"You sure this is the place?" Kelly asked.

"Just following directions," Marshall said.

"They probably told you the wrong thing back at that last place," Lauren added. "Should we go on to the next exit?"

Kelly groaned to herself. She didn't care how cute this guy was, or how much Lauren liked him. There was something strange about him, and she wanted him out of the car.

"Wait," Marshall said. "I just thought of something. Pull in at that gas station."

"Which one?"

"That one, the one with the mini-mart."

Lauren slid into the parking lot and pulled up next to the gas pumps. "As long as we're here, we might as well fill up. What did you think of?"

"The auto club," Marshall said. "I've got their card right here in my pocket. All I have to do is give them a call, and they'll send someone to get my car. I don't know why I didn't think of it before."

"That's great!" Lauren said. "Will you need a ride someplace else?"

"I'll let you know as soon as I call," Marshall said. "And don't worry about the gas. I'll take care of it."

Kelly climbed out of the car so Marshall could get free of the back seat. She watched as he walked across the parking lot to a bank of pay phones on one side of the building. He pulled a wallet from the pocket of his jeans, glanced at something inside, and started dialing.

"Maybe we can finally get on with our trip," she said.

Lauren looked up from sticking the nozzle of the gas pump into the Mustang. "Why are you in such a hurry? I like Marshall. Don't you?"

"Sure. I like him fine."

Lauren squinted her dark eyes. "What's wrong, Kel? You've been acting like Marshall has three heads ever since we picked him up."

"I don't know," Kelly said. "It's just little things." She shrugged her shoulders and tried to shake off her dark mood. She wanted to get back the excitement she had felt when the day started. "Let's just get on with our trip. You can get his phone number and get back to him later, but right now it's skiing time."

Lauren laughed. "I should have known," she said.

"You and your skiing. Don't worry. Didn't I promise to get you on skis?" She topped off the gas and hung up the hose. "You want anything to eat at this place?"

"No, thanks. They never have anything but junk at these places. I'll wait."

"Well, I'm going to go grab a soda. Back in a sec."

Kelly checked on Lauren's makeshift ski rack. So far, it seemed to be holding up fine. She leaned against the front of the car. It was chilly and the air was still damp from the storm. Despite the cool weather, a flurry of moths skittered around the fluorescent lighting at the edges of the lot. Standing there by herself, Kelly came closer to relaxing than she had in hours.

She heard footsteps and turned to see Marshall walking toward her from the phones. "Everything's taken care of," he said.

"They're going back for your car?" Kelly asked.

"They promised to get to it in about an hour, and they'll take it to a garage where it can be fixed."

"Sounds good, but don't you have to go with them? I mean, how will they get into your car?"

Marshall smiled. "It's an auto club. I'm sure they know what they're doing."

"I guess so," Kelly said. Whatever was going on, she was glad it was over.

Lauren came walking up with a can of soda. "Are they coming to get your car?" she asked Marshall.

"You bet," he said. "Everything's settled." He reached out and took Lauren's hand in his. "I really want to thank you for helping me out like this. I don't know what I would have done without you."

"Is there anything else we can do? Anywhere else you need to go?"

Marshall released her hand and sighed. "No, I guess not. It's just too bad I'm going to miss seeing my friends."

"Why's that?"

"Well, I was going to meet them in a couple of days, out in Denver. But by the time my car is fixed, they'll be gone."

Lauren's face brightened. "We're going through Denver! We could take you to meet your friends."

"I couldn't ask you to do that," Marshall said.

"Besides," Kelly added, "he wouldn't have any way to get back."

"Oh, getting back isn't a problem," Marshall said, "but I couldn't put you out like that."

"Sure you could," Lauren said with enthusiasm. "We don't mind at all."

"No, really. This is your vacation."

"Don't be silly! We don't mind, do we, Kelly?"

Yes, thought Kelly, *I mind a lot.* But what she said was: "No, you can ride with us."

Marshall gave a smile that seemed to reflect most of the light in the area. "Great! Really, you don't know how important this is to me."

Kelly closed her eyes and tried to convince herself it would be okay. After all, it was only a couple of days riding in a car. What could go wrong?

"If you're going to ride with us that far," she said,

225

"you better get in front." This time, Marshall didn't argue.

Kelly climbed into the back and folded herself into the small seat. Even as short as she was, it was cramped. When Marshall pushed the passenger seat back into place, Kelly felt like there was a wall between her and the others. The radio that had been just right in the front seat was so loud in the back that Kelly could barely hear Lauren and Marshall talking.

They were about a mile down the road before Kelly remembered something. "Lauren, did you pay for the gas?"

"What?"

"The gas!" Kelly leaned forward into the gap between the front seats. "Did you pay for the gas?"

"No," Lauren said. "Marshall took care of it."

Marshall nodded.

"No, he didn't."

"What?"

"No he didn't!" Kelly almost shouted. "Marshall didn't even go inside the store." Marshall said something that Kelly didn't understand. "What?" she called. "Lauren, can you turn down the radio? I can't hear what you're saying."

Lauren turned down the radio. "Marshall says it's okay," she said.

Kelly looked back and forth between them. "Okay? Lauren, he didn't pay for the gas. We have to go back and pay for it."

"Don't worry about it," Marshall said. "People forget all the time. Places like that expect to lose a few. They just add it to their prices."

Kelly tried to ignore him and talk to Lauren. "It's stealing, Lauren. We've got to go back and pay."

Lauren started to answer, but Marshall spoke first. "Stealing? Do you know how much profit oil companies make off of stations like that? Do you really think their prices are fair?"

"What does that have to do with it?"

"These people make billions. They don't care about a tank of gas. They have the prices so jacked up that half the people in the place could leave without paying and they'd still make money." Marshall gave a little chuckle. "Don't cry for the oil companies. If anybody is stealing anything, it's them stealing money from all their customers."

Kelly tried to stay calm. "I'm not crying for any oil company, or even for the gas station. I just want to do what's right."

"Look," Marshall said. His calm voice was really starting to get on Kelly's nerves. "It's probably ten miles to the next exit. And by then, you're going to be in the city, and it'll probably take you an hour just to get turned around." He glanced at the watch on his wrist. "It's getting close to ten now. By the time you get back here, it'll be midnight."

Kelly had to admit that spending two hours back-tracking didn't sound like a lot of fun. When she and Lauren had planned the trip, they had thought they'd make it almost to Denver on the first day. But the construction on the road, the storm, and all the running around with Marshall had put them hours behind schedule.

"I don't want to waste time, but we should go back and pay for the gas," she said.

Marshall leaned over to Lauren and said something. Lauren nodded.

"What?" Kelly said. "What's he saying?"

"Marshall's right," Lauren said. "It's too big of a waste of time to go back."

"Lauren!"

"Come on, Kel. I thought you wanted to get to the slopes, right? I don't see any snow around here." She turned the radio back up, and Kelly was again cut off from the conversation.

Kelly fell back in her seat and gritted her teeth. *This was supposed to be our spring break*, she thought. *If Lauren just wanted to pick up guys, she could have done that without leaving home or dragging me along. This is turning out to be one great vacation.*

Traffic increased as they rolled into the city. Lauren guided the Mustang between rows of trucks and cars, using the car's big engine to blast them past knots of slow-moving traffic. Lauren and Marshall kept up a conversation all the time. Kelly could see Marshall waving his hands as he explained some point, and several times she heard Lauren laughing at something he had said.

Kelly leaned her face against the side of the car and watched the lights sweep past. From the elevated interstate, the neighborhoods were laid out in neat rows. Lines of street lamps gleamed green or amber or white. When they passed the downtown area, the tall buildings were topped with flashing lights. Kelly spotted several nightclubs where people milled by the door and strobe lights beat against the windows.

She stopped trying to hear what Lauren and Marshall were talking about, and just watched things go by. She liked traveling at night. In the day, everything looked so normal, so ordinary. But at night, it was easy for Kelly to imagine that she was crossing some foreign country and the lights out there might have been London or Paris, not Kansas City.